Memories *of* Freedom

Memories *of* Freedom

JEFFREY HARDY

ISAO
PUBLISHING
PORTLAND, OREGON

Memories of Freedom is a work of fiction. All incidents and dialogue and all characters are products of the author's imagination and are not to be construed as real. Any resemblance to persons living or dead, businesses, companies, events, or locales is entirely coincidental.

2022, Isao Publishing Trade Paperback Edition

Copyright © 2022 by Jeffrey Hardy

All rights are reserved.

No portion of this book may be reproduced in any form without written permission from the publisher or author, except as permitted by U.S. copyright law. Please purchase only authorized electronic editions. Your support of the author's rights is appreciated.

Published in the United States by Isao Publishing, LLC, a division of FilmProfit, LLC. 4110 SE Hawthorne Bl., 927, Portland, OR 97214

ISBN 979-8-9875460-0-0
eBook ISBN 979-8-9875460-1-7

www.isaopublishing.com

contact@isaopublishing.com

Book Cover Illustration by Jason MacHardy

*This book is dedicated to the Nates, the Henriettas,
the Tommys, and the Martins who are still among
us every day. See and help them if you can.*

*And to all the people who came along with me, and
helped me or encouraged me to get here, including:
My wife Yuko, my son Isao, and my daughter Tomo.*

one

The closet door was ajar; the blackness of its little room leaked out, like cave breath.

Nate turned his head and started to swing his feet from under the graying sheets. He stopped, half-curled, closing his eyes, afraid to see out the window. He knew what he would see anyway. A fucking gas station. A car wash. A Jeep place. "El Guyeep" was what Lupe the brick-layer used to call them. "El Guyeep. El Guyeep." Nate wanted Guadalupe to be standing there, as full of intent as he always had been, innocent of purpose, holding his trowel loose while Nate sat on the stones with his carpenter's belt spread out around him, trying to reach Lupe's Spanish thoughts.

The dive to the sidewalk was what kept him from the window. The room was so small that it wanted to push him out, squeeze him out. He feared that he might wind up on the pavement, the excrement of his dreams and memories.

He pushed back the thin wool blankets and dingy gray sheets from his bare legs. He could dye some color into the sheets, but then the swishing Spanish boy maids would only come take them and leave more gray ones. It wasn't worth it. Nate swung his feet to the linoleum. The cold floor sucked heat from him. His butt abandoned its warmth on the bed.

Moving to the door quickly, he banished the closet's bleakness to one cringing corner. He grabbed his robe from the hook inside. It was a hint at hedonism; old browny velvet with a black collar. A Goodwill luxury. He didn't have slippers, though, and refused to wear his boots down to the bathroom. The heels of his boots were scuffed down, almost to nothing.

He sat yesterday for almost an hour, thinking about ways to repair them. His final thought was to cut discs out of wood at work. But then, nailing them on was the hard part, he would have to cut down through the seam at the back.... He wasn't going to be able to accomplish anything that way. He wanted them to last for another...who knows....

Nate reached into his jeans pocket and slipped the room key out. He pulled the heavy door back and peered into the hall. No one was near the bathrooms. He grabbed the graying towel off the door rack and ambled down the red-carpeted hall. The rug was pretty thin, but it still had enough punk to capture every stray piece of crap that fell to the floor. Nate's feet picked these things up like his soles were made of flypaper. Near the bathrooms, he stopped and leaned back against the wall. He held his foot up and brushed off the bits of collected crud. Some kind of sticky red candy, dirt, and bits of paper. As he was looking down, the door to the women's bathroom opened just a few feet from him, facing him. For a moment Nate didn't realize. Then he looked up.

She was standing there in dark blue jeans and a green shirt. Nate looked at her face, framed by burnt-sun red hair. Her eyes were staring at him, down at the foot he held up. Nate looked down. His robe was pulled open by his leg pushing out. His dick hung in there, almost in plain sight. He felt the piston move and dropped his foot to the ground. He looked into her face as he pulled his robe quickly closed. He suddenly remembered a song from a friend in school:

Nate the Natch, he sure likes Snatch.

Her skin was filled with some freckled Egyptian sunniness, and Nate noticed the delta shape of her face, her green eyes, her mouth.

The robe and towel she held in one hand, and the make-up kit in the other, she pulled to herself.

"Good morning," she said as her eyes fell again. Then she turned and moved down the hall.

Nate's robe was hung up on him. He pulled to straighten it. He watched her red hair and her rolling blue ass move down the hall. He pushed only partway into the men's bathroom. He watched her go in her room, and then her door slam, before he let the pneumatic closer shut him in.

. . .

Just like every day, Henrietta had gone into the shower with the simple little hope that it could make her feel cleaner; make her world cleaner. That was an impossible task though. This world was just too damn dirty. Henrietta fought out of the door, with all of her bath things and her robe and pajamas held tightly to her chest.

She hadn't expected anybody to be out there.

Actually, she had noticed him before down in the lobby, when she was coming in or going out, once. That was all she would admit to. She saw him.

This time she saw more than she had wanted to see. Well, at least she hadn't been thinking she wanted to see it on him. When she opened the door, he was standing there, leaning against the wall with his brown head down, in a purple robe, picking at the bottom of his feet. How could he stand to walk around barefooted in that place? She shivered. He was just wearing a robe. Was it purple? It was pulled a little open because his leg was up on the other one. She saw it just hanging there, almost in plain view in front of her. He looked up at her. She said "hi" and turned immediately down the hall, still sweating from her shower. She had to get away from there before he got some idea.

Back in her room, the towel was making her shirt damp and soaking through, cooling the skin of her breasts, still warm from the shower. There was something sensual, something enlivening about feeling both sensations at once. It made her breasts the focus of her attention. She awkwardly hung her towel on the back of the door, then let her nightclothes drop on the tightly-made bed. She started to put her make-up things in the top drawer of the dresser. The letter stopped her. It sat there on top of the dresser, next to the lamp. Her whole body suddenly felt heavy again. That brief moment of sensuality, of life, was gone again.

Henrietta didn't know why she had gone and sent Grandma her address. She didn't want her to know anything about her life now. She couldn't let her know. Grandma kept sending letters and Henrietta kept not answering them, sometimes carrying them in her purse for a week before putting them in the back of the bottom drawer, still unopened, hiding them from herself. These letters were like life trying to come back into Henrietta. She didn't want it. She didn't even deserve it. Henrietta could feel the heavy weight of her big hips and her heavy breasts pulling her down. She almost had to struggle to move.

▪ ▪ ▪

In his room, Nate watched out the window. The damp towel hung loosely in his hand. Cars were pulling into the station to fill up.

Nate caught a glimpse of sunny-topped green and blue moving across the far intersection. The red hair bounced full behind her blue-legged feminine walk. A bus squealed to a stop in front of the Guyeep showroom. It jumped and halted as she stepped up and into it. Her flash of color moved down the aisle as it lurched. She fell into a seat by the window just as the bus pulled away. Nate turned. Something like a fist squeezed in his chest. Blood was thumping in his mouth. He dropped to the bed, his robe hanging open, letting his heat escape into the air.

Nate usually went out and wandered up Mission Street on Sunday, just looking into stores. There was very little to do. Often he would go to No Money, No Honey and look for the parts to fix something. Or just to nose around in their cornucopia of junk and used hardware. The old man was usually out front, energetically trying to sell an old Hallicrafters radio or something. Inside the store, Nate always felt like he was sorting through the gleanings of bombed-out houses. There seemed to be one of almost every-thing; a tangled snake's nest of appliance cords at the doorway, old hinges, door knobs, boxes of electrical fittings, pieces of old copper pipe and old rusty tools and new tools still in the package. All of this was jumbled and tangled like a pack rat's crazy dream. It would have soothed Nate today to spend time in No Money, No Honey.

A heavy sense of loneliness weighted his mind. He wished he could keep his hotel room propped open. He wanted it to be like the door of a shop, open for business. He wanted to be needed.

A gate that needed fixing, or a door, or a table; Nate would trek with his toolboxes on his shoulders, hung by heavy straps, heavy wooden boxes clanking with tools, to fix whatever needed a carpenter's attention. He wanted to be a village carpenter and stand out in a country yard under a tree, with the sun burning the yard nearby, planing a new pine door. He'd pick a clean shaving out of the blade cup and put it in his mouth, where it would suck his tongue dry as he leaned down to push the plane into its work again.

Nate had read a book about how village carpenters worked back in the nineteenth century. He wanted a little shop like theirs, where people could come and have things built. He wasn't happy making windows for Danson, caught back in that asshole's stumble-hazard shop all the time.

Nate tried to make suggestions to Danson. Like a window he called the "S.F. Special." It was a common-sized double-hung, 32" x 60." They were mak-ing them all the time on special order. Nate wanted to build some during slack times in order to stay ahead. Danson told him to stop wasting his energy on thinking, and to put it into doing what he was supposed to do. Nate wished he had walked out on the son of a bitch Friday night.

Nate leaned onto the unmade bed. He did have a new book about Thomas Edison. He had bought it cheap on Sixteenth Street. He pulled the book up out of the bag just under the bed. He thumbed it open to the photos in the middle.

He thought of the similarities between himself and Edison. "A need to fix things" was the way he would describe it. They both just had an over-whelming need to fix things. He saw where Edison lived as a kid in Ohio, in a regular house, nothing special or big. A picture showed him as a kid with his parents. Then he saw him with his inventions and his factories and offices. Nate stopped to look closely at one picture. It was a machine that the caption said could crush rocks as big as pianos.

Edison always seemed to surround himself with big buildings and big machinery. Nate kept flipping pages. Near the end of the photographs was one of Edison in his yard in New Jersey. He was a middle-aged man. Behind him was a great big house. It looked like a fucking rich hotel. Trees were all around him. He was sitting in a chair made of tree limbs, reading a book. If Nate held his hand over the big house in the picture, all he saw was a middle-aged man reading a book. Maybe a man who liked to fix things. Nate removed his hand. The big rich house was still there. He slowly put his thumb under the cover of the book and closed it.

EDISON, A BIOGRAPHY, by Matthew Josephson.

The cover photograph was of Edison standing in front of shelves full of chemicals. His right hand propped him at a bench. His left was in his pants pocket, just under his suit vest. His face was open, and his head was wide, but his eyes were deep-set, with very little light, hiding what he was thinking.

Nate shoved the book away. It slid across the bed and fell to the floor, spread-eagled.

Nate remembered the voice of the French girl at the counter in Picaro. He almost ordered a cappuccino and croissant just to hear her say it. But he didn't have the money to waste on that. Her voice had that French self-possession to it. The French think of their language as the language of love. He liked to listen to it, but to Nate it was a language of puffery and mirror-kissing. The Asian and Indonesian languages he heard around on the street were the most beautiful to listen to; the Vietnamese and Malaysians were birds in the trees and shaking leaves in a breeze and water falling into small pools. Theirs were the languages of love.

"May I help you?

Nate looked into the French girl's face but couldn't sustain his gaze and dropped his eyes to the counter.

"What would you like? She said much louder.

He pulled the book out from under his tight arm and set it down. Warmth rushed up his face and Nate felt sweat at his hair line.

He put a five dollar bill on the book and pushed it across the counter to her. "A…a coffee, to go."

From under his brows, he searched the room for people who might be looking at him. A few heads swiveled as he glanced around. But one man by the front windows, blond, with a thin red beard, was watching Nate, looking from him to the girl and back. He held up an early Sunday paper, almost as if stopped in mid-folding. Nate looked quickly at him, then down at the counter. Twice. The blond man turned to the woman sitting next to him. She was reading part of the paper too, not quite buried behind it. Her hair was dark and neat-looking though frizzy. How did she do that? She was well-dressed, in a nice shirt with the collar up. The blond man said something to the woman again. She looked around her paper at Nate. The heel of Nate's boot began to bother him. He wanted to fix it. A tingling sensation started in his leg.

The woman said something to the blond man, then turned back to her paper. He moved his head, almost as if in agreement to a quiet joke. The blond hair picked up flashes of sun that knew Nate. Only quickly enough, the girl put Nate's coffee and change on top of the book and he grabbed them up as quickly as he could and hurried to the front. He didn't look at them as he pulled hard and slipped around the awkward door. Out on the afternoon sidewalk he stopped to breathe.

Nate reached his hand off the mattress and lifted the Edison book, letting it close properly and flop over on the floor again. He lowered his head to the mattress. His bare legs sticking out from under the robe felt vulnerable. He was unprotected. With a few contortions he pulled the blankets over his legs. It was unusual for him to want to stay in bed like this. He usually liked to get up and get out, move around. Today he just didn't seem to have any energy. Sleeping the day away seemed easier.

With the bright light of noon coming in the window, Nate pulled his pillow over his head to block the world out. If he only lifted the pillow a little, to get clearer breathing air, he would have to be looking at the dark, silent, waiting dresser. He would have to know he was in the hotel room. The light seemed to penetrate his pillow. The inside of Nate's eyelids were bright.

Nate stood in front of that store window, on Sixteenth near Valencia, near the Picaro. The window was always cluttered with funny signs and funny balloons hung from the ceiling. Nate had often seen this place out of the corner of his eye, but had never taken time to stop until yesterday. The balloons were shaped like bears and ducks and elephants. From the balloons hung little paper signs that were twisted on their strings. The signs were hand-lettered in a half-educated printing. They exhorted whoever was reading to "follow the path of righteousness", and "the way of the light." One sign read: "Work and Ye shall be receiving." Another sign, in the corner of the window, read:

> *"The fruits of our labor and world*
> *are no longer mediums of exchange,*
> *but merely commodities for speculation.*
> *Feeding our friends and our neighbors*
> *was always a source of profit,*
> *But not always just for profit from the source."*

There were so many things in the window that it was difficult to pick one and concentrate on it. Near the glass was a postcard taped to the bottom of another sign. The postcard was a copy of a Van Gogh painting. On the bottom of the card Nate could read the title. THE PLOWED FIELDS. The energetic swirling lines of the painting entranced him. The sunlight had faded the card, cutting the colors to where they were just variations on a shade of yellow. The sign above it read:

> *"The earth is the source of the beauty and bounty of our lives. To defile the*
> *earth is to defile man and to defile life and defile God."*

Nate looked from the sign to the small painting and back up to the sign again. The whorls of the sun in the painting became pinwheels in his eyes.

A breeze of hot corn husks fluttered in his ears. The heat of a southern Tennessee afternoon burned through his deep nap. Sun cut into his skin like the serrated edges of a corn leaf. A clod under his head was beginning to poke into Nate's scalp. He thought he heard, hopefully far-off, the rattle of an angry snake. He couldn't move. A breeze slipped through the cornfield and washed the heat from his body.

Nate didn't want to hoe the corn. He wanted to sleep. In his eyes were the devil's dreams of life free. He couldn't even pull the clod from under his bumpy head. He could only lie there as the sun burned him and the breeze waved corn leaves over him to ward it off. Soon, he knew, he would hear Mom's voice calling him to lunch. He would have to get up and go in and wash his hands, and sit down at the big round table in the hot kitchen and try to talk about how much he was going to get done that afternoon.

All he wanted to do was sleep here in the lap of God; or the lap of the devil, if that's who it was. His head rolled back and his eyes disappeared. He would move down the rows of corn faster than ever before. Later.

two

Henrietta saw heavy reflections of herself in the windows all around her, orange-red and green and blue. Old ladies filled the front seats, back to the middle of the bus. She sat on the street side.

At the Dolores Street stop all of the old ladies climbed out. The driver quietly fumed over their stiff-legged slowness and their poking forward with fragile fingers and canes in trepidation.

As the bus whooshed electrically away again on Sixteenth, through the yellow light, the bells in the Basilica tower started to ring outside. Today, somehow, the old ladies, and the bells, and thoughts about the age of the wedding-cake fronted Basilica, caused Henrietta to look away from the colorful people moving up those wide steps, while she in the bus moved away. They were entering a realm of Sunday security that had been denied her, entering that big wooden door. Mercifully, the bus hurried to Church Street and turned away from the ringing bells.

Henrietta got off at Church and Market. She crossed the street and headed slowly down the steps into the MUNI tube. As she crossed the lonely electricity-buzzing underground plaza, she passed a quiet-looking girl dressed nicely in purple velvet. Her hair was long, medium brown, curled under. There was a look about her fleshy pale face. She seemed innocent. Like a girl in another world.

But there was also something mutable, wild, under the girl's distant and otherworldly surface. She burned a vibrant purple image in Henrietta's eye.

Pushing through the turnstile and across another plaza to the top of the steps leading down to the trains, Henrietta heard a train beep and rush into the station. She ran down determinedly. The train was waiting when she reached the platform, humming its electric equipment song. She got in as the bell rang. The doors shut. Grabbing onto the metal pole, she eased herself into one of the hard plastic seats. As the train picked up speed into the tunnel, Henrietta's reflection flashed in the window next to her.

Deep in the tunnel, they flashed past yellow lights. She closed her eyes to control the sea of feelings washing over her. The vibrancy of a purple figure was in Henrietta's eye, and it burned darkly at the edges. She envied the girl, off to her church of sex and youth.

A fresh tear tried to wash the burning figure out of her eye. Henrietta turned and leaned to watch out the front of the train. The light at the end of the tunnel was growing.

A red brick station finally wrapped around the slowing train. Just beyond, outside, blue arched beams held up a milk glass roof. Light swept into her car.

Off to the right, houses were close to the station; little, white and snug; like paying bills every month and having someone always know where you are and when you're supposed to come home. It would be hard to get lost from that kind of life. There were so many strings attached. You would be missed in so short a period of time. "Honey, I'm home... How was your day? Did you get the dry cleaning? Is the table set? Where's the paper? Do we have enough milk for tomorrow?"

That life was full of little questions that constantly demanded answers, keeping the strings between people nice and tight. Nothing could fall off the edge of the earth. No one could just wander away, or even die, without leaving a trail of clues.

Nobody knew where Henrietta was. Nobody knew anything of her daily movements. Nobody asked her any questions. Nobody cared about her trail of clues.

The train turned right going out of the station and jerked across the track junction. It swayed a little as it moved down the street. Henrietta swayed with the car as if she were on a small ship rolling with the waves of a lonely, mothering sea.

All the houses, regular, all white or pale colors, reflected the quiet Sunday sun. All sat steady as the train passed. The train turned right and then turned again, left. Henrietta quietly rocked with the rolling motion of her car. They passed a park. On the other side, she saw a stone building with a flag in front and several police cars parked next to it. It looked like one of those friendly thirties buildings; with stucco decorations that ran across the top and around the doors in front. It was built by folks who intended it to be there for a while. They believed in the permanence of life's decisions. Henrietta's longings were to be in a place where more buildings were stone and brick, materials that demanded permanence and continuity.

Henrietta thought she had been gaining her own emerging permanence when she took the job working for Stanley. She squirmed in the seat when her mind said his name. She had wanted to stay there for a long time. She had liked Stanley, at first, and Barney. The work was always changing a little bit; filing, copying, order writing, typing, and going out every once in a while to get things for them. She had a desk that was hers and a phone that was hers and she sat out in front. Everyone came through her to get to Stanley. She felt needed in the tiny company.

Stanley didn't care about her though. He probably only hired her because she had big tits, and because he thought she was stupid and he could get her to do whatever he wanted. It humiliated her when she began to figure it out. It made her feel as if she were somehow dirty; like she had acted the way he thought she would. She hated herself for being so naïve, like a dumb little girl.

Henrietta used to be able recognize a sad maturity whenever she was melancholy. But now, a sudden gripping, pulling tide washed over her, frightening her. She had nowhere to go without a job. Her money and chances were getting thin. She constantly thought in terms of the next defeat. At every job interview she went to; even to be a waitress, or a shop helper, or department store clerk, or secretary, there were already fifty better people there before her. It was becoming impossible to wear the face of confidence she needed. How could she convince anybody?

The train rolled heavily down the hill, faster in the direction of the ocean. She didn't ring for h er stop, but let it go around the corner. For only a second, it was as if she were going to go back to town. She sat looking at her short, freckled fingers. Now they looked a little ragged. She had always tried to keep her colorless nails nice before. She sat still, feeling the jumping of the car as it bumped over something. She shivered. She wouldn't turn around to look back. A woman up front pulled the cord for the next stop. Henrietta glanced out the window. Two Chinese men were painting a house with great concentration. She jumped up and got out suddenly.

She stepped down to the asphalt, and stood in the street while the door thumped behind her. As the train rolled away behind her, she took one step toward the curb and the train rolled away behind her. The painters were covered with splatters and streaks. One of them turned his small body her way and nodded his whole head to her. Maybe it was his house. That wave of fear, or whatever it was, swept through her again. She turned quickly and walked the half block back to Taraval. The houses out here were thin-skinned. It was a working-class neighborhood deeply penetrated by Chinese and Japanese and Filipinos.

Hungry to own houses and with seemingly inexhaustible energy for work and saving money, the Asians created a large part of the tight housing market in San Francisco. Henrietta admired their constant optimism, and their ability to work and work and work.

Across 48th Avenue she started down into the sidewalk tunnel under the highway, moving toward the expanding horizon of sand and water. The roar of the surf rolled around in the concrete cavern, a steady flow pulling Henrietta.

Near the end of the tunnel, she stopped and pulled off her shoes and dropped them. They fell as if abandoned. The beach sparkled with dark mica stars as she let her bare feet sink sensuously into the fine, sparkling, sand. Moving toward the surf, the beach cooled under her feet. The filtered October beach light was almost white on the water. She had to squint her eyes so tight she almost closed them.

Henrietta kept climbing the staircase in her mind, leaning over the balcony rail, staring golden-eyed at the bright golden living room below. She left that house so reluctantly, and Mary, and Bill. She couldn't tell them why she lost her job. So she didn't tell them anything.

The first night in the hotel she had lain frozen in the bed. She tried to keep thinking about good things, about their house, afraid to go to sleep. She was afraid of who might come in. And she was afraid she would resign herself to fate and never get back out of there. The walls were almost moving with the dangers in her mind. Still, sleep somehow snuck up and grabbed her like a silent kidnapper.

She woke very early, startled, and got up and tiptoed down the hall to the shower. No one else was moving. Soap and water washed the clinging fear off. But when she stepped out to dry, and saw the bathroom around her, it began to grow again, like a mold. She tried to scrub it off her skin with the towel. She stopped. She would have had to scrub everything; from the plastic-tiled walls and the terrazzo floor and the shaggy mat she was standing on, to the walls in the hall and the chair and bed and dresser in her room, to the sheets and window and all of her clothes, and then South Van Ness Street, if she could stop there. Holding the towel over her face, Henrietta accidentally kicked the shower corner. She almost screamed. She started to cry into the fabric, naked, alone in that room.

Freezing water engulfed Henrietta's legs quickly. It soaked her pants up almost to her knees. It hungrily pulled at her feet and ankles, like a cold-fingered lover. Her heart thumped wildly. A streak of fear shook her spine like an earthquake. She almost screamed. Mary! She opened her eyes. They swallowed the ocean and the sky.

A fist of internal pain tried to tear from her throat and leap out in a cry. She swallowed it the way one would force down sickness in public. Water from her eyes wanted Henrietta to melt into the wave washing down the beach. She wanted to kiss the Pacific and swim away with it.

■ ■ ■

"Do you like to play chess?"

Henrietta blinked her swollen eyes. She remembered a man's voice. She looked Up Cliff House way. A man was fishing, and gulls were playing near the edge of the tide, like silly sandpipers.

"Do you play chess?" The voice said again.

She turned around quickly. She couldn't see clearly through her tears, but he was there alright. About six feet. Dark hair, semi-shaved face, like it had been done in some hurry in the dark, days ago. He had on two sportcoats and a pair of old, torn, grimy pants that had been blue at one time. He smiled at her. A tooth was missing from his leathered, sun-battered face.

"Do you like to play chess?"

She studied him quickly. He didn't have a game board with him. She glanced around her.

Then, he reached his hand out toward her, about to touch her arm.

A streak of panic shot through her, and words leapt out of her mouth, seemingly with a mind of their own. "If you don't get away from me, I'll put your damn eyes out!!" Her voice was so threatening and sure that his face immediately went stony, and his hand stopped, almost touching her arm. She reached into her purse without taking her eyes off him.

His eyes moved to her hand, watching it search the bag. His curling fingers pulled back as he shifted to turn away, his face hollowed, hurt. "I only wanted to know if you like to play chess." He pulled back from her, mumbling, then turned and shuffled away in the damp sand, down the beach, past the tunnel he must have followed her through. Henrietta would have laughed if she could have laughed. She looked up the beach. The fisherman was packing his gear. She glanced sharply back to be certain that the other man was gone.

People in a knot were running down the hill from the highway above, carrying beach things, hurrying across the chess player's shuffling path. The sky had gone momentarily golden, through the light fog. Down the beach, two surfers were walking into the sunny afternoon surf together, about to paddle out. Tears pushed again into Henrietta's eyes, but they weren't the deep tears they had been before. She laughed after a moment. At herself. No, not at herself. Maybe at him. Or at the fucking stupid ocean. "Fuck it,

God! Fuck it! Fuckit!! Fuckit!!" The world wouldn't let her swim forever in the ocean. No! She had to fight off chess perverts. Or was it chest perverts? She laughed.

The ocean air brushed across her face. Where tears had left tracks on her skin, it tightened. She squeezed them out and relished the breeze, swinging her head and throwing her thick red hair behind her.

Her stomach gnawed. Henrietta looked around, up and down the beach. That guy was far down there now, talking to a woman lying on a towel. Brave; lying on this beach like that, in the cool air, and with folks like him around.

Henrietta turned back from the freezing water and began to move back up the sloping beach. When she got to her shoes, she reached down and lifted them, feeling a little like an old woman picking up one more thing somebody dropped and left as she makes her rounds through the house at the end of the day. Henrietta trudged up into the subway, still barefoot, her wet pants cooling her legs. She was preoccupied; watching the floor of the tunnel, noticing the patterns of the sand blown into it in miniature wave rows. Some held people's and dogs' footprints, like memories of their passage.

At the other end, not watching, Henrietta almost collided with a large Chinese family. Her heart started to beat rapidly as they surrounded her. There was an old lady, two sets of younger parents, and a gaggle of Chinese children. It looked like it could be four generations. Henrietta stopped in the tunnel as they swept around her like a small wave of unnerving pleasure. After they were past her, and the children were let loose, to run squealing through the tunnel, she stood still for a few moments, experiencing the exhilaration of all that wonderful human contact. She put her shoes back on and hurried to the train stop on light feet.

On the bench, she watched the Chinese men down the street, still painting, diligently, and quickly. Henrietta almost thought she could hear their voices. She was calmed by just sitting there.

Another pair of voices, musical, came around the corner and up behind her. She turned to see two older women with well-worn shopping bags on their arms. Their language sounded like a blend of Spanish, something like

Japanese or Chinese, and every once in a while, a startlingly clear word in English. The result was beautifully musical, like tiny rippling waves at the beach. The sound of their voices was so entrancing, she just closed her eyes and listened.

three

Nate's eyes slapped open to the sound of a siren passing below his window. He almost jumped up. It didn't matter though. Just another one. There were so many sirens in a town like this. Poor people with heart attacks, or pulled from car wrecks. Poor people with houses on fire, or maybe someone who'd committed a crime. Sirens were all bad news.

He refused to look at the clock. It didn't matter what time it was. It was time to get up.

Nate pushed himself out of bed, and he did see out the window, as the siren kept going, out South Van Ness. Across the street, a car was pulling out from the car wash, to be dried by the swarming teenage kids. The moving car window caught the sun just right and it flashed into Nate's window, just like somebody had flashed a sirening spotlight on him. He almost backed away from the window.

If he was going, he better get outside as soon as possible.

. . .

Nate stepped from the elevator into the lobby. There were a few guys sitting back in the corner, watching football on the TV. Nate only glanced their way as he turned. He completely ignored Benny behind the clerk's window.

Nate's uneven boots clumped on the linoleum. His heart was suddenly heavy with the prospect of being out in the street alone, unprotected.

Out the door, he looked down the sidewalk, toward Sixteenth, where two guys were leaning on the wall outside Kenny's, sharing a bottle. Nate sped up past them, trying not to stare. He turned the corner.

Just around the building, an old man shuffled past Nate, dressed in an old seaman's faded clothes; a light blue shirt that was thin as gauze now from so many wearings and washings, and thin denim pants that had become a whitish blue. Nate had to pull himself short to keep from running into the slow-moving figure.

He turned to watch the old man, who stopped at the curb, half-bent-over, like something was wrong with his back. His hair was all white, and had a wispy quality to it. There was nothing unclean about him, but he obviously had trouble taking care of himself, shaving and things. He probably lived all alone. So many old people lived alone.

Nate's breath stopped for a moment, like he was in the loving squeeze of an old woman's arms. He almost bent down, mimicking the old man, as if he too had something wrong with his back. An Eastward breeze blew down Sixteenth Street, across his back. Nate wanted to taste the salt air in his nostrils. His heart carried too many years for his body to remember at once. His feet moved on the painted steel deck of a ship. The slow roll of the water put him in a slow-motion dance. He wanted to turn and taste the wind of the sea fully on his lips, to see further at that moment than anyone else could see, with his body rocking under thoughts of the sky and where he was going, and the god of his body going there free.

The old man stood at the curb, unsteady, as if he wanted to reach out for something to hold on to. Nate moved reluctantly, trying to hold himself upright in spite of his back, and in spite of his feet not being in time with the balance of his body. Nate needed a brace, to hold his back straight and to keep his body in flow with the movement of his feet. He wanted to make a wooden brace that could hold the spine in the position it was meant to be.

It would take a couple of leather straps around the torso to hold it in place, but those were no problem. And if the wood was finished smooth and curved just right it would almost feel like he wasn't wearing anything.

four

The wound cried with jiggling pain at every step. Tommy wanted to turn back. He felt like a roast of meat on a fork being shaken onto a cutting board. He had his neck tilted up, staring at the light on the pole across South Van Ness.

Finally, it popped to green, with a clicking thump in the metal box. Tommy looked carefully around before he stepped off the curb. He had to fight his legs all the way across the street. Getting old gives you a lot to be pissed off about. But it's the legs that usually go first. Walking is like slipping down a slow, sloping beach toward an undertow.

Before he was up at the other side, cars squealed away behind him. Tommy had to stop, just on the curb, and lean with his hand up the light pole, his eyes held tightly shut. Even though it was just on the other side of the gas station, the clinic seemed almost too far. But if he got something for the cramping tear in his back, this might all be worth it.

. . .

As if through watery prisms, Tommy was seeing several of things, five windows superimposed over each other, and they were all sideways. He lifted his right arm a little and moved it. The skin of his arm rubbed the loose skin of his torso a little. At least it felt alive. He tried to move his left arm but it was pinned under him trapped, from his shoulders almost down to his hand. He blinked his eyes clear. He could see the tower and Twin Peaks. He had been sleeping on his side. Never, as long as he could remember down his 66 years, had Tommy ever slept on his side. And damn these hard hotel beds. He flopped onto his sagging-skinned back.

"God!! Cocksuckers!! Goddammit!"

His lower left back streamed fast and hot with pain. He gathered all of his strength, grabbing the sheet in his left fist to pull up onto his side again.

"Fucking little Chicano Cocksuckers." Tommy wanted to sing himself back to sleep. He wanted to sleep until the pain was gone. Bells on a church nearby rang. Tommy raised his eyes to his watch on the table. Probably the Mission. Hell. He knew those fucking bells. He'd spent his share of Sundays over in the Basilica; sometimes at the Spanish Mass. He'd often let the large, opulent church melt happily in the singing voices around him.

Now he was all alone in his mind with God.

God! The deserter of old men. The God that protects tormentors of old men. Tommy wanted to heave in and heave back out with a dramatic rush of unhappy air. The tape on his back and side, and the stitches, wouldn't let him. Tommy closed his eyes. He wanted off Sixteenth Street, and out of this town. He wanted to be back over water, floating, happy in the stainless steel kitchen of his life. From water Tommy knew he had come. When he died, God please help him, back to water he wanted to return.

. . .

The sooner he got something for the pain, the sooner he'd feel better. Tommy pushed off the pole and got his feet moving again.

He and a girl in a car danced a halting shuffle at the exit drive of the gas station. He tried to wave his arm, but the scream of pain in his back caught his hand in the upswing. Anyway, the young blonde girl, so small in her big blue sedan, insisted he pass first. It seemed an interminable time to him, crossing in front of her. He watched the sidewalk a couple of feet ahead of his shoes, wishing he had the strength to flash her a winning smile and a young man's wave. Tommy had always drawn looks when he was dressed in his going clothes, all neatly pressed, with his heavy bag on his shoulder. He used to move on his gimbal-legs in a way that said he was going out! He knew he didn't look like much now. He didn't even glance back to watch her pull out.

There were so few things in the neighborhood still familiar. Well, familiar from any time gone. Nothing was as it really had been. Tommy refused to reminisce. But he did allow himself to feel like a stranger in his home city. There was very little that was his anymore.

By now, he had probably been gone more than he had been at home. He had spent many years with his berth moving with the whim of the moon and the roll of the waves.

Tommy remembered a friend from growing up. Frank O'Leary. Frankie'd been a boatwright on the waterfront, when they were still needed. Then later he'd opened a cabinet shop, across the street, about three doors down Shotwell.

A car had popped Frankie through the window of the New Mission Cafeteria a few years ago. He landed in the middle of one of those tables of old people. He was old himself, dead on their table, soft. Somebody probably screamed.

Frankie'd been Tommy's best friend at home; always there, always the same. He and his wife used to have Tommy over for dinner. She was nice, but quiet, and pretty as a soft Irish lamb. Mary. She was always so quiet. But very polite, and waited on you. She took an overdose of pills. Then Frankie.... To hell with it. She was gone. Frankie was gone too.

As he passed next to the fenced lot behind the clinic, Tommy lifted his head. The gate was padlocked. There was only one car in there. He slowed, but turned the corner and approached the entrance. Wouldn't there be more than one?

Tommy made it to the large mural painted on the wall. He passed it, uninterested. He was almost afraid to look at the entrance. The glass doors were closed. There was no movement behind them. There was no receptionist at the curved desk, and no one passed down the hall that ran behind the desk.

Tommy read the legend on the doors.

MISSION HEALTH CENTER
Centro de Salud
de la Mision
Horario: Lunes-Viernes 8AM-6PM

"Goddam Chicanos! Don't those son of a bitches have enough of their own shit around here?" Tommy caught himself and looked around. No one was out on the street to hear him. He turned back toward the doors:

Informacion: 552-3870
Citas Medicas: 621-1152

"Why don't these assholes learn English if they want to live here?" He learned their goddam language when he lived down there.

Tommy had always loved the Mexican and Central-American people, but things were getting out of control; knifing old men in the alley outside their hotels, and everything in Spanish, everywhere. All of the government agencies were filled with these people now too. They were probably the ones fighting to keep their friends from having to learn English. Try calling the city sometime. Half the people answering the phones, no shit, don't understand English! So you have to say everything three or four times. And you can't understand what they say. They want to be able to vote, so all the damn ballots have to be in three languages. Maybe four. He didn't remember about Japanese. But at least the goddam Japanese seemed to want to be a part of the society. Maybe all of those years of goddam revolution in Mexico and Central America had bred something into these people. And this mural on the wall; with naked women and giant flowers and people with their hair on fire. What the fuck kind of art shit was that?

Tommy leaned his butt slowly down to the fender of a parked car and stared through the clinic doors. Now he had to go all the way back to the hotel. Anger knotted in his throat, threatening to constrict his breath. The air rattled in his chest before he let it slip out. The last bit pushed out a sob. Tears came to his eyes. He'd never cried so much in his whole life.

Except after Dolores jumped... From the top floor of the hotel where she worked. From the top...down to the jagged-glass-topped wall by the swimming pool. Tommy always had to fight to keep from imagining the Acapulco sky flying down with her, collapsing with a balloon sun onto the burning beach in front of those cringing white towers.

She still had the goddam dust rag in her hand.... He was sure he would have had a son somewhere now. Her family wouldn't tell him anything.

He would have married her. He would have tried. At least he wouldn't have let the baby go uncared for, without money.

But money wasn't why she killed herself. She couldn't go back to Rebecca's with a baby. And she couldn't go back to her family. What other man would want her? Some people have tremendous fight when they can see what they want, but then no fight at all when it gets too crowded to see. Tommy had replaced the dry, acceptable certainty of her freedom at Rebecca's with the crowd of too many possibilities.

Her family wouldn't let him into her funeral. So, Tommy took a cab out to the Pie de la Cuesta, just like they used to do so often together. He got out, almost alone on the beach. It seemed strangely still, windless. He fought across the sand in the new shoes and suit and flopped into a hammock under the giant palms, and just watched the heavy brown waves rip at the wide beach, exposing layer after layer of sandy new skin. Drinkless, he just hung there. The crocodiles in the lagoon back across the road kept entering his mind. He imagined one lunging out of the water and sliding across the gravel and down the sand, to sit under his hammock, hard as armor on a boat. He knew if he moved the hammock, or let his hand fall, it would drag him out and tear him to shreds.

Tommy hung quietly until sunset came, until the sky flamed, a sweeping furnace of loving pastel fires, burning everything to purity. Tommy cried for absolution, throwing his guts out into that furnace to burn clean.

He lay in the hammock long after the fires were out. Then he went back into town, up on the hill, to the house. He feared his life could be in danger from one, or all, of Dolores's brothers. Out a corner of the bedroom window he could see the town all lit up, out on the point. The fun of life didn't stop for some people. Tommy threw his sea bag in the middle of the depression on their bed. The whole time he was stuffing things into it, he kept look over his shoulder. He hurried out of the bedroom and almost tripped on the rag rug lying near the door. Dolores had made that rug from old clothes. One of his old blue shirts and an undershirt were in there. A smell of her came to him, and it burned from his nostrils down his gullet into his middle. He tripped again on the rug as it clung to the rubber soles of his new shoes. He tried to carefully shake himself out of it. A big knife was hanging on the wall over the sink and cooker. She had used it so deftly, for cutting machaca, and almost everything. A lemon tree was outside the window, its waxy leaves still in the hot dark, and the perfume coming through the window, deepening a terrifying ache in him. The plywood floor squeaked under his impatient feet. Tommy grabbed up the rug in a hurry as his shoulder pushed the screen door open and he stepped out into the prickly night. The light from the middle of the room outlined him on the ground. Tommy put his bag down and stuffed the rug into it, then slipped his hand through the door to pull the string. In a hurry then, almost tripping over it in the dark, he grabbed his bag again, and moved quickly through the streets to find another cab.

five

Passing La Cabana, the door opened and two couples came out laughing. Nate thought he could smell warm tortillas and the carne asada on a grill. He thought about going in to eat, but he was going to the T&M again. Chinese food is cheaper.

Out on Mission Street, by the BART, there were small crowds on all the sidewalks. Groups of Latinos bunched on the street corners and other somehow appropriate to them, public places.

Someone yelled from a clot of young guys out into the street.

"Amigo!! Que paso?!"

From a passing car came, "Hola Eduardo!!"

Nate joined the conversation, to himself, in his own style of Spanish. "O nada amigo. Y con usted? Que pasamos mis amigos que muy bueno y los tardes muy mucho todos mis amigos muy que buenos zapatos." He pretty much exhausted his little store of Spanish.

At the corner of Mission, he glanced down the street, and upstairs on a fire escape, hanging half-in and half-out of the window, was a young man with a guitar. He was striking the perfect pose for a Latino on a fire escape in a window with a guitar. Nate could almost believe it was a photo he had seen somewhere. A friend, also out on the fire escape, was striking the perfect pose for listening to his friend's guitar, as if at any moment, a group of young girls would walk by and look up and notice how perfect they were, and want to climb up with them.

Nate spoke to himself again. "Hola! amigos. Hola!! Hola!! Hola!!" He felt like marching up the street to a Latin beat.

He looked back down. Two teenage girls were coming toward him. Nate's scalp suddenly tightened. One of the girls brought fire to the eyes of every man she passed. Every man's head turned to follow her. She had a little fat girlfriend with her. Maybe her shield from the flames erupting all around her. Her hair was black, wild, like a mountain storm, and her pants were black and tight. Her shoes were flat and brilliant red, and her tight-knit shirt hugged her, red as her lips. When she got close Nate could see into her eyes, black as panther fur. He could only breathe hot, shallow breaths.

Red and black. Death and blood; brooding, danger, night. Sex on the street. The pot always simmering, sometimes boiling over. She was every girl every man had ever known; all mothers and sisters and daughters, all waking up at once. She was every woman they wanted, but couldn't touch. She passed near Nate. He felt the heat glowing from her. Just a touch of her fingertip would have burned a mark on his skin.

He almost tripped on the bad heel of his right boot, turning to watch her, feeling clumsy as she passed. Her face was sleeping and volcanic, about to erupt flaming at her lips. Nate rippled with a tingle of fear as he stood, conspicuously, to watch her go by. He couldn't help himself though. They all turned too. A pain in his chest was a last nail, just driven into place through a board over a door or window, throwing a lonely room into total black.

His head went back down, and the sound of the sea swept up on him from the right. Mona. Soft, in soft slacks, khaki, and a soft sky-blue blouse, climbed on a bicycle and turned from him. The Pacific, to his right, was schussing and calling. She was on her bicycle. If he raised his head he would only have to watch her pump away from him, so sure she was right to leave him there, gagging on his thoughts trying to shape words.

A chill sang through his whole body. Nate shook his back to throw it off. He was almost sure he wasn't crazy, nearly hallucinating, but the fear could still rock him and make the sidewalk watery under his feet. He wanted to hurry to where he knew something or someone. Inside. Where he could become engrossed in something. Where he could forget himself. He could almost just stop and cry; right here on the sidewalk. But then he would be out of control and totally alone, with no one to help him to a home he couldn't even articulate. They would put him in a hospital. He might never find his way back.

The light was green. Nate pushed himself across Mission Street. Half-blind, he looked down the other side, beyond the BART plaza. In front of a bar, he saw a small Filipino-looking man who stood, as if he was hiding, behind a power pole. He wore dark sunglasses and stood quietly, close to the pole, watching something intently. Nate couldn't see what he was watching. Backed to the wall, spread down the side of the bar were four women. One turned to the others and made a joke. They all laughed. Nate wanted to see them closer. He angled across the street, down that way.

As he came up right near them, one of them called. "You want to party?"

Now he knew. They were the Filipino guys working girls. All four were dressed differently. The first one was black, in a gold and black dress. The second was a bony blond-haired white girl in a pale pink halter top and white shorts. Her shorts were smudged, probably from leaning. She was the one who spoke to him. Nate looked her in the eye, but he couldn't see past the blank window of her glassy stare.

"Come on. Let's party. I'll make you glad." She didn't sound excited about it. The words were as empty as her eyes.

The last two were Hispanic girls. The contrasts of skin on either side of her made the pale blonde seem whiter still. Nate glanced from the skinny white girl to the two Latin ones. They were almost as young as the little sex volcano he'd seen across the street. He started to turn his head to see where she was. Instead, he searched his pockets with his mind. He didn't have the money, but he wanted to buy the dark ones. All three of them. He wanted to wrap himself in the dark, moving clothing of their skins. He wanted to be a snake in their deep, shaded, garden.

Half-embarrassed, Nate turned around and headed back toward the BART plaza. Behind him, the black girl pushed off the wall and her red shoes slapped on the sidewalk behind him. Nate swung his head quickly, to glance back at her. She merely pursed her lips, bored. The sharpness of her eyes seemed to be a challenge as if she was wanting to be talked into something. Maybe like running away with him. Nate kept turning back to see her, but she was only changing her location. In the background, he saw the pimp in dark glasses lean off his pole, looking intently, sharply; straight at him. Nate turned back around and headed on.

Ahead, a small group was gathered on the train station plaza. At first, he thought they were all just waiting for the bus. Then he saw something move strangely. His chest began to tighten. Nate knew how small incidents in the Mission could often find a way of escalating themselves. He stayed near the edge of the plaza. In the middle of the commotion was a crippled Indian, with a walking cane. He looked like a wino or a bum. His pants fell in tatters on his shoes, much too long. His hair, stringy, greasy, and matted lay on the shoulders of his distorted jacket.

six

Sometimes, the way he turned his shoulder into oncoming people, with his bad leg behind him, Martin felt the sleek and perfect grace of a buck deer, carrying his head importantly, weightily, forward. The sidewalk was clumped with people. It would be clear for a few yards or so and then another group would be standing and talking, or dancing and listening to music. There was an aching temptation to swing his stick and scatter some of them. Nearby, two old Chinese women, in their Chinese shoes and those flappy jackets were leaning against a paper rack, probably waiting for the bus. A couple of teenagers moved into Martin's way. They were Hispanic brats, wearing clothes that should have been on their big brothers. They danced at each other, mock-boxing, trying to interest a pair of giggling girls standing at the phone booth pretending not to notice. Another boy, watching the boxing, had a large radio cradled in his arms. It was playing salsa music loud. He was fat and quiet, brooding. He wore a net over his hair. He was growing one of those soft-hair mustaches that teenagers have. The two boxers shuffled in front of Martin, without seeing him. Their heads were down, with their hands up, flicking them into each other's faces. Martin stopped. He almost brought his stick up and cracked the closest one on the head. He held his hand and stood, steady as a hot dry stone, waiting for them to notice him, almost between them. He spoke in a low voice. "Get the fuck out of my way."

With these kids, there was only one kind of masculinity. You always had to be ready to fight. They weren't altered by the anger in Martin's face. Martin was bulkier, but all three were about the same height. His stick started to leave the ground. The fat kid turned the radio quickly off and piped up, "Hey Pancho. You and Roberto Duran!! Can't you see this guy's a cripple?"

Martin whipped his head around to the fat kid. His eyes flashed like fire up on a lone-pine mountain. He moved to raise his stick further but stopped in midair. He threw the stick to the ground, pulling his hands up in front of him, striking a pose to box. "Fuck you, sissies. I'll show you boxing. Come on! You too, fatso!! Come on!!"

Martin's hands waved around his face like smoke clouds around a burning mountain. His fists were flat, big enough to be menacing.

His strange footwork, hopping toward them, and then limping clumsily to the side, made the two boxers laugh with each other. The fat kid kept his radio turned down a moment longer. He almost laughed too. "He's just a fucking crippled bum Pancho. You guys let him alone."

The two kids turned away, both of them sneering their lips up, like angry twins. Martin wasn't impressed. He wanted to kick some ass.

Martin was no young buck in his first fighting season. He'd seen plenty before this, and he could still swing what he knew. They didn't like moving for him, but they knew under their skin that he would take them. He reached down and snatched up his stick. The hairs on the back of his neck weren't standing. There wasn't anything for him to fear. Martin suddenly knew the power it took to show his back to his enemies.

seven

The Indian's stick seemed to be a strange, weak thing as he swung it around in the air, jabbering and walking away from what looked like a near fight. A pain cut through Nate's chest. He could hear a crackling scream deep in his ear. A bird's scream. On the inside of his blinking eyelid was a bird's jumping eye. Nate stood on the curb, quiet, entranced, as the Indian came shuffling his way.

A bus suddenly squealed up to the stop. Two Chinese women who had been leaning, waiting, suddenly shoved in front of everyone else to get on.

Nate watched the Indian step rhythmically past, using the walking stick to aid a bad right leg. He turned and watched him move up toward Seventeenth, slowly, even gracefully. That black prostitute was leaning against the corner of the first building. She looked harsh and hard.

Nate spun around. A creaking cackle in his head echoed deep in his ears. His body turned sideways to push into the sidewalk traffic. Half of him was a great strong wing. The other half was something withered that he had to drag with him. He wanted to grab the fearless strength of life back. He glared ahead, pulling powerfully with his good side, dragging the weak half with him.

eight

Martin turned on Mission and shuffled almost half a block. A tall black woman leaned at the corner of a building. She wore a black and gold dress high on her thick and meaty legs. Her sandals were red and her lipstick was red. She had red globes hanging from her ears. Her hair was straight and arched stiffly over her head like it belonged on someone else. When she turned, trying to get a new leaning spot, he saw the knot in her dress, tied up to reveal even more of her long and heavy right leg. Her skin was dark and thick. She looked past him, bored with him. She thought he didn't have money for her. She was wrong. He knew what it took for her! His nose was an eagle's beak, and his eyes were an eagle's eyes. His head carried the antlers of a buck. His body had the loose fleshy strength of a bear. He wanted her to climb his dick like a pine-nut squaw and squat on top, squeezing him with her scratchy feet.

"Move on Tonto. Before you put a cramp in my business."

"What if I am your business?"

"Shit! You?! I don't want your business."

"Keep going up the street pal."

A Filipino had just snuck up behind Martin. He pushed him in the back with a bony fist. Martin tried to twist around to confront him, but his shoulder was suddenly grabbed by a sturdy hand. The guy wasn't big, but he had strong hands. Martin tried to shake him off, but his arm barely moved, like talons had his shoulder pinned.

The hunting whistle of the eagle is a high-piercing sound of warning, a cry of anger and hurt, almost like the need for food is a result of God's unfair distribution of power and pain. The whistle gives a fair warning that there is no selection of justice in the food chain. We take what we overpower, and run from what can overpower us. There is little chance for the small ones, the ones who can't dive down to snatch in strong talons what their eyes pick from the grass.

The whore wasn't even looking at him as he was pushed, lurching, down the sidewalk. The gripping hands released him and he started to turn back. Immediately, he felt the shock of a small fist jabbed in his neck, thrusting him forward again. He had been singled out; no chance to find the freedom of his own strength, his own movement, his own gait. His fucked-up leg was a second personality that he carried with him, usually unaware. He was reawakened to its limitations. Martin became smaller in his own mind when he grasped the true nature. He tried to move quickly, to leave the realization behind him in the groups on the sidewalk. He tried to visualize the confident soaring of the eagle, to feel it in his body and in his legs.

Martin hated to be driven by fear. He tried to kick the ball of fear out of the half-buried lodge of his consciousness. It hit the door frame of his mind and dropped just inside, to lie there like a warning stone tossed by some god. Martin looked up, to read the sky.

He should have seen a circle of turkey vultures overhead, their slow, looping, patient wings reserving energy. Vultures are friends of death, black, circling messengers from beyond. "Paging Mr. Little Foot. Message for Mr. Little Foot". Look up and see their big wings and the little red heads and your entire body moves. They look down and see you and their gullets constrict a little and their tongues swell and tighten in their beaks.

Martin stopped just the other side of Seventeenth Street. He leaned against the gated front of a car repair place. The pigeons overhead should have been vultures, circling with messages of more than one death. The street corner was moving with people. The pavement was throbbing with cars taking people somewhere after Church or bringing them out in the afternoon. Some on foot were heading down toward Sixteenth, probably into the BART stack, into the new working machinery of the earth.

Martin spotted a likely pair. "Excuse me. Can you spare twenty cents, so I can leave town?"

The couple stopped. The man, blond and red-bearded, with small, piercing eyes, reached into his pocket. He pulled out a quarter and put it into Martin's palm, cracked and dark from dirt and constant exposure.

The man's face was inscrutable but didn't seem put out. The woman was pleasant. They were clean and looked healthy. Her dark hair was curly, and well-kept. Her clothes were extremely neat. They kept moving, with only a quick stop and the contact of eyes.

Martin thought he heard them laugh to each other.

"That's great. Twenty cents to get out of town. I couldn't pass it up."

The woman asked. "Did you see that face?"

"Great huh?"

"Great face. Fuck you, Charley, and Mrs. Charley. What the fuck do you know about shit? Fuck heads don't even know I was fucking them off. Everybody wants you to get out of town. And for twenty cents you'll get out just for them. Ha! Fuck off!!"

Martin turned and headed for two guys and a girl coming from the other way. They looked like the kind of people who were always boycotting something; always in solidarity with something. Wearing baggy sport coats, with little knapsacks over their shoulders; they all three had on the counter-culture shoes, Birkenstocks, with corduroys or jeans.

"Can you help me get to Seattle? To find my family? Anything would help."

They all stopped and went into their pockets, looking at each other. One of the guys, with a new-starting beard and an earring in his nose, spread change in his hand. It was a lot of pennies and some other coins. He took some out. "For the bus." He dumped the rest into Martin's palm. The others did similar, but the girl counted what she gave before she did, wanting to make sure it wasn't too much, or too little.

"There you go brother." The first one said, and they all looked Martin in the eye as he dumped the money into his grimy jacket pocket.

"Thanks. May the eagle of strength fly over all of your heads."

There was a return in unison; in their voices, if not their exact words. "And yours, brother."

Martin let them pass, and was already looking for the next hit. When they were a few feet away, he growled after them. "And may he shit in your hair as you walk."

Martin learned panhandling by watching pros. Panhandling was a game in your mind. It was a way to get over on the assholes. While you were asking for money, you were really fucking them off for spending so much time thinking about it. But they weren't smart enough to figure that out.

The best mindfucker was a woman named Elizabeth. She was black and big, and wore nothing but all black all the time. She was big enough to jam the doorway in Macy's downtown. The first time Martin ever saw her, she was sitting on a bench, with her bags squatting next to her, by the new convention center. The air was hot and kicking up scraps of paper and stuff and dropping it again on everything. People were crowding toward the convention center. As they passed her in a stream she yelled into them. Martin watched from the middle of the moving people.

"Give me a thousand dollars. Give me a million dollars!! Give me a million billion trillion dollars!!!" Her voice was an angry gospel singer's, and she was lashing out at the waves of her listeners. "I don't care!! Give me a thousand trillion dollars. Now!!! I know you have it!!!"

She just sat on the bench, fat, her fat bags next to her on both sides. She wore a black coat and a black hat, about the shape of her head, and she rocked, almost angrily, shoving her hand out on the end of a straight arm for emphasis.

"Give me a million dollars and I don't care!"

Not many threw money at her. But some did. She just sat, not moving to pick it up. She set Martin free. She was the loud echo by the river of their lives. She was dropping their thoughts back on them like a well-thrown fishing net. She was free of them. She fished them proudly as they passed.

"Give me a thousand million billion trillion dollars. And hurry up!!! I don't care!!"

The last few words came out almost as spit. It peppered over the passing flow like a river-splashing rainstorm.

Martin never hung around long after panhandling. He usually went up Mission. Up there, he could eat some Mexican food and go into a bar for a few beers. He knew better than to go into a place down here where somebody might recognize him. They could get pissed at him. And this was the easiest job he'd ever had.

Once in a while he'd get a bottle after dinner. Most of his friends liked Christian Brothers. The little brown brandy bottles were all over town, in weeds next to the sidewalk, in doorways, in gutters. The Christian Brothers. Martin had seen their fancy factory up in Napa, once. He was hitchhiking, and got stalled for two hours, right across the road from it. Everybody stopped to take their families or their girlfriends in there, like it was a wine Disneyland. He found a piece of paper in the dirt by the road. It told how they ran the wine business to help in their work. What work? Providing little bottles of brandy that were handy for drunks to put in their coat pockets and take behind a dumpster somewhere?

Martin missed a few customers "Fuck them!!" He was getting off the street anyway. They were starting to give him the willies.

nine

At Church and Market, in the shade of a building, Henrietta was hit with a breezy chill. But it was always that way in San Francisco; cold in the shade, warm in the sun, misty in this part of town, sunny over there, gray with fog over there.

Henrietta used to look out on this intersection every day, riding the "J" home from work. Her stomach churned as she began to think about Stanley again. It just came on her. She didn't want to think about him. Stanley Steinberg. The memory was a bath of bubbling insults.

When he invited her to one of the house parties that he always talked so much about, she really felt privileged, like she was becoming part of something.

She was impressed by his house as she stood out front. It surprised her that he lived on Upper Market Street, so near the Castro. She didn't care, but it made her wonder what sort of man he really was. The house was one of those fancy Victorians, painted mostly dark blue. The other dark colors she couldn't tell in the night light.

She was glad to be there, and felt finally accepted; even a little special. She rang the bell. The man who answered the door surprised her. He had on a leather mask. Feathers from the side of the mask swept around his head, into his gray hair. He was wearing leopard spotted tights, no shirt. She was shocked, but tried to keep it to herself. He was tall. He pulled her in by the hand. He leaned down so she could smell him, like some kind of old Egyptian she thought. He told her in a hoarse voice that the party rule was to leave one crucial piece of clothing at the door. Behind him, on a couch, was a pile of discarded clothing. She could feel heat in her neck and cheeks. She laughed, but not as loud as the party's noise. Henrietta lifted her foot to offer a shoe, trying to cover her embarrassment with humor. Stanley must have snuck up behind her.

"Henrietta! I'm glad you made it!"

She was immediately relieved. She turned to Stanley's familiar voice for help. She was surprised. His face was covered by a blue plastic mirror mask, with the word **STARFUCKER** on it in little red rhinestones. Her heart jumped into her throat, almost choking her. All he had on was a red jock strap. She tried to catch her stumbling thoughts for a moment. She glimpsed the party in the other room, as these nearly naked, sweating, men crowded in on her. One woman in there was totally naked, except for her mask, and two guys had their arms around each other, wearing leather pants with no backs in them, their hairy butts out for everyone to see. She couldn't remember what else she might have seen in that quick look. Stanley talked into one ear, in a voice he must have thought was smooth and persuasive. The hoarse man was bent to her other ear. Stanley grabbed up a feather mask from a basket behind him, asking her to put it on. Then she felt someone's hand on her right breast. The hand squeezed her. She jumped back, out of instinct. She didn't know which one of them it was. She apologized, "I'm sorry, Stanley," and backed out the door with her shoe still in her hand.

In the summer night, the light air blowing across her body made her cold, moist with fear and embarrassment. She walked quickly back down Henry Street to the "J", and rode home. Exhausted, she snuck into her room, not telling Mary and Bill.

Henrietta knew to be afraid of going to work Monday. She was right too. Stanley wasn't nice to her when he came in. He didn't talk to her. Later in the day he asked her why she left, and she told him that she just couldn't do that. She just couldn't. He accused her of being self-righteous and looking down her nose, which he said was "too fucking big" anyway. She couldn't say a word without starting to cry. So she didn't.

The very next day after that, coming back from the bathroom, she passed Barney's workroom and Stanley was in there talking to him.

"I really thought she might put out. I wonder who she thinks she's saving those big tits for? Nice and soft, too. I copped a feel of one…real nice. I think she's just playing a game with me."

Barney used to joke with her sometimes, while he was packing shirts, when Stanley was gone. But he only talked to Stanley if he had to. Barney told him, "I don't think so Stanley. I'd just let her alone."

"You don't know anything about women Barney, I do."

Henrietta hurried quietly to her desk before Stanley came back out.

The next day he fired her. He told her she was wasting his money. She didn't ask him how. She wasn't going to give him the satisfaction.

She tried as much as possible not to think about him now. If she thought about him she'd want to spit on him. She hoped he went out of business and had to move back to New York, or Rhode Island, or wherever he came from.

Henrietta crossed Market Street to where the buses stopped. She was waiting for the 22 Fillmore to take her back to the hotel. She stood on the sidewalk, outside a bar. She didn't look into the windows of the bar. It was gay. She just wasn't interested in seeing what they were doing in there. Guys kept coming and going, in pairs and threes, wearing leather jackets, and jeans, and heavy black boots. When she first moved to San Francisco it had been interesting a little bit. She was curious about them for a while. But the novelty wore off fairly quickly, and now she just felt it was silly, and sad; all of those men sitting in the window, looking out for someone to come along. It was like one of Stanley's sad parties.

Stupid, she wanted a MUNI train to go by while she waited. She could remember riding it out to the end of Church Street. A lot of nights she used to stop and get something for dinner at the meat market.

Henrietta looked up and the "J" train was coming out of the tunnel, about to turn toward her. A 22 bus suddenly pulled around the corner up the street, just as the train veered into the bend to head down the tracks toward Henrietta. Her heart started beating, like they were in a race and she was the finish line.

It was strange. As if they were truly in a race, the "J" car lurched forward for a brief moment, seemingly to get the jump. Henrietta impulsively hurried across the roadway to the train island. She didn't know why.

The train did get there first, and when the doors opened, she hurried up the steps, showing her transfer. She swung herself into a seat behind the driver. The bus pulled quietly up next to them and gave a blasting hiss from its brakes. Her heart almost skipped a few beats. It was stupid she knew, but she was going to have a look at the old neighborhood, just for fun. Maybe she'd eat in a little restaurant up there. She sat up straight, in anticipation, as the train lurched up Church.

Just past Sixteenth, where the 22 bus always turned toward Mission Street, Henrietta began to watch everything intently. She loved the front of the big school near Seventeenth; beigey stucco, the entrance decorated with Spanish tiles. She wished she had gone to a school that pretty. Hers had been a little farm town school. A county school really. Flat and boring; nothing but brick and windows. A place you wanted to get out of as soon as possible. She would have liked going to this school.

What she liked most was where the train cut behind Dolores Park. As they climbed the park's grassy hill, the city fell open below, and Henrietta could see all the way to Berkeley. The park was a sloping green berm; splashed with people in the sun, some chasing the October sun. Away across the rooftops, the hard-edged buildings of the city couldn't touch her.

The car wound up the hill, taking curves with graceful slow ease. Henrietta was part of a sinuous animal, crawling.

At Liberty Street an older woman got out, and Henrietta quickly crossed over to her abandoned seat. Next to the tracks, behind a wall, up a small hill, was a mansion of brown mottled stucco. It sat quiet, seemingly whole unto itself. Big ferns grew in the garden, next to the house wall. Steel gates were closed across the driveway. Red-flowering trees hung out over the sidewalk above the high retaining wall. The train pulled forward and the house disappeared behind a high wall, painted the same mottled color. Henrietta always used to wonder what it was like to sit behind one of those big arched windows in that house and look out over the city, quiet and insulated. She craned her neck but the house was obscured by the wall, protected from her eyes.

Henrietta pushed from her mind the fact that she was riding the train on Sunday; for a lark; as a reminiscence. The car was nearly empty, but that didn't convince her she wasn't with other after-work riders. She faced out the windows tiredly, anticipating the restfulness of home.

They made her feel at home. Masters made her feel at home. He let Henrietta pet him and feed him. He came to greet her when she pushed open the door in the evening. Bill gave Masters to Mary when she finished her degree. He named the cat. Mary liked the reminder of her status.

Sometimes Mary would be sitting in the big front room when Henrietta came in the door. Masters would be in Mary's lap and would jump down to greet Henrietta. He would walk her into the living room and jump back in Mary's lap to purr. Henrietta would sit close to Mary and pet Masters while they talked quietly about the day. Bill usually didn't come home until later. By that time the women had gone up to their rooms upstairs; Mary across the balcony, and Henrietta down the side hall to the back.

Henrietta would sometimes stand at her window, to watch the sky show its colors over Twin Peaks, before sitting on the bed to change clothes.

After cleaning up a little she would go back downstairs and help Mary fix something for dinner. Masters would rub against their legs while they cut up chicken. Even if his food had just been dished out, he would leave it to rub against their legs and beg for some. He made even more of a fuss, meowing for fish or squid. Those meows had their effect. Mary was the stiffest to his begging. She would mildly scold, in a voice that only played at discipline. "You've got your own bowl of food over there mister. This is for us. You're mighty friendly when we're cooking."

Henrietta would always cut one of the pieces of fat skin from a breast and say, "I'll just give him this. You don't want this on yours do you?"

Mary would look at Henrietta. "You're an old softie, aren't you? You can't take it. He knows who the susceptible one is around here." Masters would rub against Henrietta, turning back and forth under her feet.

The train ground to a halt. "Army Street."

Henrietta hadn't even been aware of the other stops. She jumped up as the door thumped open, and hopped down the steps to the street. After the train left, she crossed Church between cars, still half-believing she was on her way home after work.

Henrietta stepped briskly up Army.

At Dolores, she stood on the crest of the small hill, and gazed out over the Mission District and the front of Bernal Hill. Down Army, she could see the big warehouses; and past them, across the bay, Oakland. Sun glinted at her from the window of a house way over there. She turned toward home; the first house just around the corner.

The wisteria that draped from the trellis above the garage soothed her, as always. Henrietta hurried across the edge of their driveway.

Her foot was on the first gray-painted concrete step, when she stopped. She hadn't even got up to the wood ones. She glanced up expectantly, at the cream and white face of the house. The door was set back, painted a golden color, protected in the vestibule.

Henrietta wanted Mary or Bill to come out the door and bring her up the steps and welcome her in, knowing that she came with nothing.

Henrietta stopped on the second step. She turned and hurried back to the sidewalk. This was a stupid game she had started. She turned back for Army Street but stopped again, confused. She spun once again and hurried up the hill toward Twenty-Sixth.

Henrietta pushed herself up the hill. She tried to move faster with each step. Halfway up, as she passed a hedge that leaned out over the sidewalk, she thought, for a stupid moment, that she heard someone call her name. Adrenaline pumped into her blood. She moved faster.

Henrietta thought she heard her name again, but ignored the hallucination. She kept herself to a tough pace on the hill.

Something suddenly grabbed at her arm. She turned to throw it off, thinking it was a tree limb or something.

"Henrietta!" It was Mary, panting from the chase on the hill.

"Henrietta?" There was almost a question of identity in Mary's voice. She seemed impatient. "Henrietta! Wait a minute!!"

Henrietta stared blankly at Mary's face for a moment, almost as if it was a dream. She didn't want to acknowledge something that wasn't real.

"Just wait a second, would you, Henrietta?" Mary bent over to catch her breath. She held Henrietta's arm tightly.

"Hi Mary." Henrietta tried to keep her voice natural. She tried not to show her fear.

"Henrietta?" Mary was concerned and still out of breath. "Bill and I have been worried about you. Since we hadn't heard, we were beginning to wonder if you were alright, and where you were. We get mail for you but haven't known what to do with it. We couldn't get any information from the phone company, if you had a new address or what?" All of this came spilling out, one piece on top of another. Mary wanted to get a lot said and her breath would only barely allow it.

She looked good. Henrietta noticed her hair was cut shorter, around her face. Her clothes were crisp and sharp-looking as usual; even on Sunday. Henrietta had always admired that about Mary. She had thought being around Mary and Bill would rub off some of that good, organized life on her. She really tried for that. Somehow she didn't have what it took to do it. She just didn't understand what she had to do to get there. Henrietta tried to smile at Mary.

"Why don't you come on back down to the house and we'll sit and talk."

Henrietta lied. "I'm in a hurry. I was just going by. I thought I might have a second to stop and say hi. But then I knew I didn't. So I kept going. Maybe I could pick up my mail later on. Some other day?"

"If that's what you want to do?"

Mary was bewildered now. She wanted to get Henrietta down to the house. Henrietta knew it. Disquieting fears about the way Henrie was dressed, and the way she was keeping her hair, ran through Mary's mind. Henrietta knew that. She could see it in her eyes.

"Your grandmother has been trying to call you. She called two times this week, trying to find out if we had heard anything. She said you weren't answering letters at the box number you gave her. I think she really wants to talk to you about something. We have a couple of old letters from her up in your room.

That last was a fire arrow thunked into the wooden wall of the fort of her heart. Henrietta pulled lightly, to get her arm out of Mary's grasp. "I really can't now Mary. I have to go meet somebody. Maybe I'll come by this week."

Can you tell me where you're staying? I'll call you and we can meet for lunch, if you don't want to come to the house?"

"It would be better if I called you. What's your number?'

"Henrietta! What's the matter with you? It was your number too. Don't you remember it?

Mary tried to look into Henrietta's eyes. "Are you sure you're alright? I'm worried about you."

"Everything is fine. I'll call you this week and we'll see about lunch."

"Are you sure I can't call you? Do you need a ride somewhere? If you're in a hurry?" Mary trailed off.

"No. I like to walk. But I've gotta go now."

"Okay. Call me. You promise?" Mary wanted to grab Henrietta's blank green eyes with one of those powerful stares that extracts binding promises. Her soft brown eyes, under her too-neat brown hair, didn't have the power.

Henrietta pulled away from Mary and turned up Dolores Street.

ten

Tommy's nose and chin itched where drops of salty water gathered. He reached into his back pocket for the bandana. Many washings had made the patterned cotton soft as a hand full of flour. Tommy wiped his whole face with it. He had only a twitch of pain in his back as his hand moved up and down.

"Are you okay mister?"

The voice was kindly inquisitive. The accent was deep Spanish.

Tommy lifted his head. There was a young Mexican man. He looked Indian. His face was wide and flat, and seemed concerned. A few feet behind him was a young woman, quietly round and pretty. Her face was inquisitive too. She held the hands of two children who were half-hidden behind her. All were dressed as if they had just come from church.

Tommy blinked his eyes and wiped his face again quickly.

"Perdon?" he asked.

The man laughed. "No amigo. What is your problem?"

"Nada. Nada. Yo...uh...I was just remembering something."

"You are remembering something very sad my friend. Could I be of any assistance to you?" The man's voice was thick, deep, honest.

"No. I was just here to go to the clinic. But they're closed."

"Are you sick my friend?"

"No. No." Tommy hesitated. "I got cut up the other night by some...by some kids. I just wanted something for the pain."

The man made a face as if he completely understood. He looked back at his wife and children, then turned to Tommy again. "Perhaps you would like me to take you to the General Hospital?"

"No. No. That's not necessary. I think if I just get back to my hotel room I'll probably feel better. It already hurts less now. Maybe I just needed to get out and move around a little."

"Are you sure I can't take you to the hospital? My car is right across the street." He looked close into Tommy's face and pointed.

"No. I don't think...I need to go now."

The man turned back to his wife again for a moment. "Then I will drive you home at least."

There was such sincerity in the man's face, and concern in his voice, that just as Tommy started to protest, he relented. "I won't be taking you out of your way? It's on Sixteenth Street, just past Mission. The Altamont Hotel."

"No amigo. It's no problem. We were going that way."

The children peeked around their mother at Tommy, their flat faces like dark dreams of innocence. The man took Tommy's arm to help him off the car fender and out into the street. The woman and her children followed.

Tommy sat uneasily in the front of the car. He held his left side turned out from the seat. He pushed both of his hands rigidly into the cushion, protecting his back from the bounce of the car. The two blocks seemed to stretch much further. Traffic had become heavy. Tommy felt impatient. On the dashboard in front of him were two little statues; one of the Virgin Mary and one of Christ with his hand raised in absolution. A thin piece of palm frond was looped behind them. The family rode quiet. The children strained to understand why this man was with them. They leaned forward from their deep seat, to get a good look at Tommy and be aware of all his movements. Their father sat upright, half-turned toward the children and his wife, and half with his eye on Tommy and the road. The wife sat in the back, quiet, as her husband negotiated through the tangle mess of cars.

Tommy's back didn't hurt as much as he had thought it might. In fact, he felt better than earlier, even with the constant jumping of the stiff car in traffic. Still, all Tommy wanted was to get out.

The car crossed Mission Street and neared the hotel. Tommy turned to face out as it described a small arc. He pulled the handle a little too early and the heavy door of the Chevrolet swung open under momentum. Tommy didn't even try to stop it. When the car halted, he turned sheepishly to the driver.

"I want to thank you for the ride. I was feeling...." Tommy stopped.

"For nothing my friend. It was only a little thing."

Tommy glanced at the dark, beautiful family in the back, then back to the man. "Thank you anyway."

"You have a good day amigo."

"Good bye now. Adios. Muchas gracias." The Spanish came easily out of Tommy's mouth.

"For nothing, my friend. For nothing." The man leaned way over to help Tommy close the heavy door. A car behind them honked loudly. Tommy felt like yelling "screw you, asshole." He kept quiet.

When the door thumped shut, Tommy stepped over to the curb. He turned and watched their little car, the wife's head just barely over the top of the back seat as they made their way off again. On the sidewalk, them gone, Tommy suddenly realized he didn't want to go back up and lie in his bed. He'd spent enough time alone up there. He wanted to be out. He was sure he could sit at least for a little while. He turned toward the T&M.

Standing in the open doorway of the restaurant, Tommy swung his head back and forth, looking across the tables, trying to find a face he knew. The place was nearly empty. A youngish couple was near the door. How many people around here did he know anymore? He tried to think of names, but none would come. Maybe he was losing his memory. Tommy spotted a table where someone had left a Sunday paper. Suddenly, he felt he was in a race. Tommy surveyed the room as he hurried toward the paper. No one else was moving.

He let himself into the chair cautiously, wincing. He glanced around the room before looking at his prize. It was open to the opinion page. Tommy ran his eyes over it. There was a column on the bilingual ballot. He sort of sympathized, but wasn't sure exactly how he felt about that right now. He had absolutely no interest in an article against condominium conversions. Tommy was long past being able to worry about that. Over on the spine of the page was a column called THE QUESTION MAN. Tommy squinted at it. Pictures of people were next to their responses to a question asked on the street.

The second picture seemed familiar. Tommy looked at it closely. He read the name. Ethel Harris. Ethel! It WAS her. He used to shack up with Ethel between trips when he was in his early twenties. Jesus Christ! Forty years ago! She had been a sweet thing. She wanted to tie him down to some kind of work where he wouldn't be gone all the time. During one of his trips out, she found someone else. Tommy never did know his name. Must have been this Harris guy. He wished there was a picture of him. She might not even still be married. Tommy shifted his eyes to the answer under her picture.

"Marriage seems harder sometimes when you're younger, and you don't have all the money you need, or think you need. But when you realize that this is someone you can always count on to be there when you need somebody, it gets better and better as it goes on. I'm very happy for our forty-five years."

Tommy quickly glanced at the question at the top of the column.

"WHAT ARE THE GOOD AND BAD THINGS ABOUT MARRIAGE."

There were several other pictures and answers. Tommy didn't have the stomach to read them. It was something about Ethel's answer; about seeing her changed picture.

As Tommy looked back across his life, it was like he'd just experienced a string of meals or something. Some were good, some were bad, and some were great, as long as they lasted. His memories of beautiful women were only like memories of meals. Suddenly, he felt imprisoned by the bleakness of what he had not done with his life. He hadn't saved anything, anything of his life; anything. No one had ever told him how it should be, what it would be. His mother hadn't known how to hold onto things, make them last. His father had left before Tommy even knew him. And that stopped his mother in her tracks. She had tried her best with Tommy, but she hadn't known what to do after his dad left her, he was sure of that now.

There had been times when Tommy hoped he might see someone who looked like the picture his mother had kept on the dresser. He would have thought she wouldn't want to be reminded, but something there must have been stronger than any pain could erase.

There was no chance to hold onto, or save, or nurture anything now. Now, Tommy was supposed to be the one with the knowledge to pass on. But he was just like his father probably had been near the end; all alone somewhere, with no one to tell anything to.

Tommy was tired of thinking. He turned and stared at the wall next to him. In the grain of the blue-white paneling he could almost see the outline of an old face, someone like his mother. And she looked like Ethel in the photograph in the paper. Only older. Tommy looked back down. The photograph of Ethel had become blurry in his vision. He stopped trying to look at it.

eleven

When Henrietta got to Church Street, half-out-of-breath, there was a train coming, heading the wrong way; away from town. But she wanted to get on it, in case Mary tried to follow her.

She knew she'd only been fooling herself, going by their house. Now she'd gotten Mary all upset.

Sitting in the train at Twenty Sixth, a little blue car pulled up fast, right beside them. When it was right under Henrietta's window, she could see Mary's agitated face in the driver's window. Mary's eyes were searching all up and down the street. Henrietta could only see Bill's leg and his hand. Lucky, Mary didn't look up and see her in the window, there hadn't been time to get out of the way.

Mary gunned her car at the same moment the train lurched forward. Henrietta stood up and watched as Mary yanked her M.G. dangerously across them and made a quick left down Army and back toward Dolores.

Henrietta closed her eyes, just for a moment, to let everything go past. She only wished she hadn't gotten Mary all going like that. Too much was happening too fast, and she wasn't in control.

After she knew they were gone, back in her seat, the world left Henrietta for a moment. It was pleasant to sit in her little seat and feel the sensations of the train as it rocked its way off Church Street.

The feeling shot out of her just as quickly as it came, though. Like she couldn't relax for a moment. Henrietta quickly reopened her eyes. The train was almost across from Soon Lee. They had put a new red awning up. It stretched over the sidewalk, with big white letters on it. The thought of shrimp and snow peas almost made Henrie's stomach growl. She remembered times that she and Mary and Bill had gone up there when they were too tired to make dinner. It really wouldn't hurt, she thought, if she got off here. They wouldn't still be searching in the neighborhood. Henrietta pulled the cord and the STOP REQUEST lit up.

She got out at Twenty Ninth and eagerly crossed to the restaurant.

They had put new stained-glass doors up. She pulled one. It was a little heavy.

Just inside, Henrietta waited, half-hidden behind Chinese evergreens that topped a chest-high partition. She could smell the warm welcoming odors she had remembered. There were no other customers.

They had completely redone the place. The walls were painted Chinese red. The upper part of the walls and the ceiling were fresh white, and they had put in new track lighting where there had been fluorescent strips. Little painted fans with angel fish on them were tacked to the walls. Chinese paper accordion lanterns hung from little brackets all around the room. Henrietta was brightened by the color. She could never understand how the Chinese did it, how they could mix colors like orange and pink and pale blue and yellow and green. Henrietta just hoped that all of this new stuff didn't do anything to the prices.

A small skinny man, Henrietta didn't recognize him, came out of the kitchen. He looked at her quizzically, then raised his hand high in the air, waving her to come in. Henrietta hesitated a little, before she skirted around the partition. She stood again, wondering whether they were open for business or not.

"Do you want carry out?"

"Oh. Are you closed?" Henrietta was confused.

"No. No. Would you like to sit anywhere?" He swept his arm around the room, indicating that she could take any table she chose. Henrietta's eyes swept the room, confused by all the choice. She settled on a little table against the wall, near her. She started to move that way.

"Would you like sit here?" The little man hurried up to the table.

Henrietta nodded her head and sat down. He hurried away, to get a menu Henrietta presumed. She only hoped she hadn't made a mistake. It was so comforting though, to be sitting in here. Maybe it was because they used to come here a lot. Maybe it was the safety of the family neighborhood. Maybe it was because she was going to be actually waited on, instead of being treated like a piece of meat that had just stopped in for a cheap meal. She hated those cafeterias and lunch counters down near the hotel, and the crazy, dirty people. She had become so tired of that.

He scurried over with a menu and left it at her elbow. Henrietta opened it. She was right. The prices had really gone up. This neighborhood was getting richer all the time. The stores and restaurants had to get in with it. Soon Lee got with it. Henrietta had enough money with her. But she felt guilty about spending it, with only a hundred and fifty dollars left in her drawer at the hotel. She had no idea when she might get another job. Or even if she would. The government didn't seem to care. Not with its new way of thinking about people. Jesus! Wasn't she a person? Wasn't she allowed to eat too? Wasn't she allowed to feel good for a moment? Even if it was her last good meal, she was going to do it. $6.95 for Sweet Peas Shrimp.

Actually, this was nice. It could be kind of like her own personal party. She was going to get all of the attention. Henrietta heard the laugh of a child and she turned around. There was a little Chinese girl running back and forth, back in the doorway of the kitchen. She had a tiny paper kite in her hand and she was making it fly behind her. Henrietta suddenly felt smothered in family warmth. She looked around again, at the warm red walls and the new red tile floor and the colorful lamps, and the fish fans. She felt temporarily content.

twelve

Nate was dragging a wing and a foot behind him, like a grand wounded bird. He was tired of all the obstruction. He longed to jump from the earth and use his wings to fly. He tried to envision a mechanism that would enable his bad wing to work the drafts in the upper air. What natural forces made the complications of flight suddenly simple? Weren't bones just sticks and hinges? A hard obstruction grabbed and trapped Nate's feet, throwing him forward. He grabbed frantically, without seeing. He found a thrusting arm that he tried to hold to and balance himself.

Someone shoved their hand into his face and pushed him, screaming, "Why don't you watch where you are going!!" It was a woman with a Middle-Eastern accent.

"Are you drunk and something? You are irresponsible person!" She pushed again at Nate, hitting his arm. His vision cleared.

At his trapped feet, a dark-haired boy sat in a stroller. The boy's big round black eyes stared up at him. To keep from falling on the baby, Nate had to roll off to the side. He fell against another old woman who was trying to get by and almost knocked her down. She yelped and jumped out of his way. Nate tumbled, with nothing to stop him. When he hit the hard sidewalk, the baby started crying.

The woman behind the stroller screamed again. "You bum! Should not be outside drunk, with babies and women walking! You belong off street." She took off, shoving her strolled in front of her like it was a battering ram.

Nate didn't have a chance to answer her. People stepped around him, glancing down, sure he was drunk. No one tried to help him up from the bricks.

Nate pushed himself off the ground, and stood up, taking a brief inventory. The heel of his left hand hurt. It was one of those skin scrapes where you see the tiny red dots of your capillaries. The new skin was very light and pink, surrounded by dark, work-stained, older skin. His left knee hurt a little too. His pants had a thin, white spot where the fabric had gotten scraped on the plaza. Everybody skirted around him, looking him over critically.

Nate had never been drunk a day in his life, except once in the seventh grade. He'd learned all he needed to know about drinking from his dad, Johnny Ring, who was drunk just about every day that Nate ever knew him. From the time Nate was nine, until his dad died when he was nearly thirteen, if Nate wasn't home before Johnny and Corrine went out drinking, near dark, he was locked out until the bars closed and they came home at three in the morning. If he was cold, or hungry, or tired, too fucking bad. He slept under people's porches, or scammed money for sandwiches, or hung around with whoever in the neighborhood looked like a good prospect to cadge into something.

The old bastard died drunk too, trying to get back up Bernal Hill from the 3301 Club one night he went out drinking by himself when Corrine was home sick in bed. Nate had only been back from Mom's for two nights, and was staying as far away from Corrine and her puking as possible. The police found his dad lying at the bottom of the concrete playground slide, next to the shortcut stairs between Prospect Street and Winfield. He had to walk if Corrine couldn't drive him, because they had taken his driver's license away again. Who knows what the fuck the stupid shit had been doing on the playground?

Nate sure didn't want to have anything to do with Corrine, and she didn't want to have anything to do with him, so they took him to a shelter right away. Nate really wanted to go to Mom's farm. But he knew he would be a burden to her. He had never wanted to leave Mom's, but he didn't tell her that. It was clear she was slowing down. They wanted to put him in a foster home until things could get sorted out. Fuck a foster home, though. Nate snuck out of the shelter the next afternoon and cut out of town without giving them time to think about it. He hitched to LA, where Jimmy, his older brother lived; and where they kept his mother in the crazy house.

She'd told Nate they put her in there for knifing somebody in a grocery store. It made him depressed to visit her, but he went every week while he lived with Jimmy. She was so pretty. Her hair was black and she had that smooth coffee South American skin. She was beautiful. Nate thought she looked like some kind of a queen, the way she sat there in the bed, propped up like she was just at home, being pampered or something.

Nate wound up looking like his father. Like an Irish dock hand, with dark red hair and freckles, and light skin that had gotten a little darker from being in the sun too much, working on houses. He was taller than his dad had been, but not much. Fucking stupid drunk. Nate wondered if it had been because of his mother that his dad drank. Nah. His father was just a drunk, and his mother was a crazy. She died in the hospital. A black woman knifed her. His mother always called black people niggers. She wasn't too bright. Sometimes Nate thought it would make him understand how his mother was if he went crazy. Even if it was only for a little bit. But he was so afraid, he could never do it.

Mom had never been afraid of anything that Nate ever knew. At least not when he was with her. She used to go out and kill rattlesnakes in the chicken shed with her twenty-two. And she'd go way down in the low pasture, across the creek, where there were more rattlesnakes, and cotton mouths, and bring her two cows home in the evening. She used to crawl under the house in the cobwebs, where Snippy just had fifteen pups, and bring them out so Snippy couldn't drag them off where they would die in the woods or become wild. The only thing Nate ever saw Mom afraid of was a black man who came up to the house one afternoon. She sent Nate out to the door of the screen porch and told him to find out the man's business, but not to let him in. Mom stood back inside in the living room with her shotgun ready for anything funny. She just didn't trust black men. Maybe that was kind of normal for growing up in Memphis. That's where his father got it. But his mother grew up in Brazil. He wondered if the hate had rubbed off on her from his dad.

One year, when Nate was eleven, he stayed in Memphis a good bit of the year. Mom put him in a Catholic school nearby because she went to church there. Nate remembered her sitting next to him in that big church, with her black dress on and her little hat with the black veil. She was at least four inches shorter than him, even then. She had a round face, and it was starting to get all wrinkled. Her mouth pursed up as she said her prayers with the Mass. The church smelled like the incense they burned in the Mexican magic stores on Mission. Nate didn't watch the priest much. All he really wanted to do was go back to sleep, or go back and eat some of Mom's pancakes, or play on her pump organ, or look at the collection of Indian arrowheads and skulls and bones in his grandfather's old dusty desk in the cluttered, unused office.

Nate was suddenly frightened of what could happen to him in the short span of a moment's time. His whole life could instantly change. There was no one to help keep it the way it was, where he could trust it or believe in it. He was totally alone in the world. Totally alone.

Nate hurried across the BART plaza, headed directly for the T&M Restaurant. He wanted to be in there. He wanted to be where he could sit and eat and just be quiet and not disturb the world, and not have the world disturb him.

He zigzagged across Sixteenth, hurrying between cars that honked their horns at him. He dashed in front of a parked car, behind one pulling in. He was being dangerous.

He shoved against the glass door and stopped just inside, where the green and beige linoleum had been worn away by thousands of passing feet, exposing the original black and white ceramic checkerboard underneath. All the high walls were sheeted in white-washed, electric-blue paneling. Dusty Chinese scrolls relieved the monotony of the pale blue every six feet or so. Around the top of the room, the couple of feet that the paneling didn't reach, the walls were painted bright orange.

At the first table, a woman and a man, both in their late thirties, were talking intently over cups of coffee. She had stringy brown hair. Her skin looked to have been over-exposed. She was making a speech, as if she wanted to convince herself as well as the man. "I tell you, this time I'm gonna stay clean. I'm getting a job, and some nice clothes. I'm gonna take vacations every year back to see my sister and her family...."

Her voice was still droning when Nate got back to the glass-fronted steam tables. There was no reason to look at the menu board. The $2.50 chow mein plate was almost all noodles, but it always filled him up. Nate glanced back at the little Chinese man now there, standing only a little higher than his steam tables. Nate nodded in recognition. No words ever passed between them, too easy to confuse, so Nate pointed at the Chow Mein.

With another pair of traded nods, Nate took the heaping, steaming plate off the glass top and slid his tray to the cash register. Another silent Chinese man waited there, nodding too. Each stood, hands held behind his back, until a customer came into their section. After serving the customer they stood back again, serious with their responsibility, their hands behind them again. Nate got an iced tea, paid and turned.

He surveyed the room, looking for the right place to sit. There were ten or more tables free, only three in use. One, by the inside wall, had an old man sleeping at it. Nate decided and headed straight for the front windows, like he was in a hurry, keeping his eye on the slippery tray. Halfway to the front, he noticed that the old man's leg had spread out across the aisle, about to trip him. Both the iced tea and the chow mein scooted toward the front edge of the tray as Nate slowed down and he had to dip under it to avert an accident. He snapped his head toward the old man, almost angry.

But the old man didn't lift his head. Nate chilled with the quick thought that the old fart was dead. He leaned down to brave a look, and recognized the old sailor he'd seen at South Van Ness. Nate set his tray on the corner of the table. It made a loud clack on the hard surface. The man's head started to move.

"Hey mister. Are you okay?" Nate dropped down to a squatting position.

Tommy looked into Nate's face. His eyes were blurry from sleep. He was grateful for that short retreat from the pain.

"Are you feeling okay, sir?"

Sir? Jesus, Tommy couldn't remember the last time someone had called him that. Probably some young girl in an office, asking him to fill out papers or something. This kid was maybe in his late twenties. He could have been a little older, but looked younger really. He had that Irish-angel look that would never go away. His face was heavily freckled, and his hair was reddish brown, with a little wave in it in the front. The wave kept falling down in his face and the kid kept pushing it back. He was medium-sized, a little thick, as if he had come from stock that could be bigger. Tommy opened his mouth to speak. Moisture had collected there while he was asleep. A bubble formed on his lips and broke, sending tiny cool sprays of water onto both of them. They both wiped their faces at once, in reflex.

Tommy tried to pull his foot back quickly. A grimace twisted his face.

Nate realized he could have let the old man sleep in peace. "I'm sorry. You really look like you're in pain."

Tommy grunted. The pain wanted to come out in a loud groan. Tommy grabbed the edge of his seat, to keep from exerting his back muscles. "You're right. Somebody could have got hurt."

"Is there something I could do? Did you hurt your back?"

Tommy hesitated, then decided to tell him. "I got cut up a bit by some kids the other night. It gives me hell when I stretch the stitches."

"Christ! Where...?"

Tommy pointed. "Right in that alley out there. Like a dumbass I tried to take the short cut up from Fifteenth Street. I didn't want to miss the game opening on TV.

"Do you know who they were?"

"Sure I know. I saw them. But I don't know who they are. They...." Tommy looked around the room before he went on. "Fucking Chicano kids. Little coward twerps. One of them decided to slice me across the back because I didn't have any money. Isn't that the shit?"

Nate screwed up his face. "Jesus. That must have hurt. Did the cops come?"

"Cops? Shit. I stumbled out of the alley out here to the sidewalk until somebody going by finally stopped. She yelled and somebody called an ambulance."

Nate glanced quickly around toward the serving counter. "Could I get you a cup of coffee, or something... For waking you up?"

The old man waved him off. "No. No. I don't need anything. Don't pay any attention to me. I'm just an old shit, complaining. Your food's going to get cold. Probably is already."

"Nah. It's fine." Nate started to put his hand on the tray, as if to pick it up. "You sure I can't get you anything? A cold drink?" Maybe a glass of iced tea?

Tommy realized the kid really wanted to do something. Somehow, it would make him feel better. "Okay. Yeah. A Coke or something sounds good. Maybe it'll wake me up."

"Great! I'll be right back." Nate hurried to the counter. The Chinese man served him, then returned to standing, spread-foot, with his hands behind him.

Nate hurried back and set the Coke down in front of the old man. He eyed the paper. "Do you mind if I sit here and look at your paper?"

Tommy looked up into Nate's face. "It's not my paper. I just found it here. I guess it's okay with me." He wasn't completely sure though. Sometimes the young guys in this part of town could be sort of strange. Especially the ones eager to make friends.

Nate reached his hand over the tray of food as he sat. "My name is Nate. What's yours?"

"Tommy." Tommy shook the hand.

Nate was hungry. He lifted his plate and glass off and set the empty tray on the inside chair. He dug his fork hungrily into the noodles. Cold, the grease that they had been cooked with began to congeal. They weren't slippery anymore, but clumpy, glutinous.

Tommy sat and watched. He took a big draw from his glass. "Thanks for the drink."

Nate talked around the food. "Don't mention it." After a bit, he looked up from his plate. 'Do you live around here?"

Tommy made a face. "Would anybody hang around here if they didn't have to?" Tommy didn't give Nate enough time to formulate an answer. "If you want to call it living, I'm over at the Altamont. Almost next door."

"Yeah. I know that place. Next to the laundromat. I've never been in there. It's nice inside, isn't it? I've seen the brass elevator from the sidewalk."

"Nice? It's just like all the other hotels like that anywhere in the world. They're all the same." Tommy shrugged a tiny shrug, remembering his back.

"You been a lot of places?"

The kid was gonna pester him with questions. Tommy nearly rolled his eyes. "I guess so. I've been around the world probably thirty…ahh…maybe twenty-five times at least, I guess."

"How did you do that?" Nate looked at Tommy's clothes. "Were you in the Navy?"

"Merchant marine. I've shipped all over. Almost everywhere more than once. Well. I haven't been to Alaska, or to the North Pole. Or Russia. I met Russian sailors though. I wouldn't sign on ships going to really cold places. I liked South America, and Australia, all over the Pacific; Japan, Malaysia, Hong Kong. Mediterranean, England. But my favorite places were in South America and Mexico. I like the people down there. I can speak some of the language. I love the women. But right now, all I can do is look at them, until my back heals up. I guess I'm getting old."

Nate twisted his mouth down to say that he didn't believe Tommy was old.

Tommy recognized the look. "I am. Just a few months ago, in June, I turned seventy-two. A little over two months ago. Almost three. No four."

Tommy's face showed a lot of weather. Nate could imagine him on the deck of a ship, keeping watch in the night. "You lived here, though?"

"Well. Some of the time I did. I was born and raised here. But for a while I lived in Mexico." Tommy fought the old pain in his chest. He wished it could have been gone forever by now. He swallowed the words. "In Acapulco."

"I grew up here too. My father worked on the docks. He was a stevedore. I'll bet he unloaded your boats. I've lived in other places too. In Memphis, where the paddle wheel boats were. Well. I didn't ever ride one. They were a long time ago. I lived in Los Angeles, and Carmel and Monterey for a while. Now I'm back here."

"It sounds like you like to be near water too."

"I never thought about it. But I guess I do. I've always lived pretty close to it."

"Yeah. Acapulco was my favorite place." Tommy looked away, out the window, like he was watching something, but he couldn't see anything except Sixteenth Street, cars and people. Tony, a little Italian guy from his building, passed off a little packet to a skinny black guy at the edge of the alley.

"You lived in Acapulco?" The kid sounded excited.

"Yeah. It was my favorite place. I lived there for about a year and a half once. Around Nineteen Seventy. You know. It was a little off and on. Because I had to ship out and come back. But it was my favorite place to live. The weather was good. The beaches were nice. And you could lay in a hammock all day and drink for almost nothing. You'd just lay out under a grass hut on the beach and they would bring drinks down to you. You didn't have to move a muscle. The women were beautiful. God, they were hot little things. Like hot peppers. They call them Chiquitas in Acapulco, in Mexico. Those Chiquitas were hot stuff." Tommy laughed to himself. He moved in the seat a little bit, and tried not to groan too much with the pain.

Nate reached over to help, but there was nothing for him to do. His hand hung in mid-air until Tommy stopped moving.

"I remember the first night we were ever in Acapulco. A cab driver took me and a buddy up to a place called Rebecca's. It was up on the top of the hills, overlooking the bay. Bahia de Acapulco. It was off of Calle del Morro I think. Anyway, when we got out of the cab and walked up to that big house, we could hear music. And there were people on the veranda dancing. When the car doors closed, there must have been about fifteen girls came running across the patio to us. They were like birds flying out of a jungle. They all wore different colored robes and things. The moon was big and bright. I remember seeing those girls as plain as day. They were running up to us, singing like jungle birds. 'Pick me. Pick me. Pick me.' It was like something I might have dreamed about, or read in some book. Shit. 'Pick me. Pick me. Pick me.' I couldn't believe it! But it didn't take me long to pick the girl I wanted. She just came right out of the crowd and grabbed me by the arm. I guess she picked me. I wanted to handle all of them, like they were pies at Thanksgiving and I wanted to stick my finger in all of them, even the ones I wasn't going to eat. I put my hands around the waist of one, and tried to feel the tits on another one. But this girl took me by the arm. There wasn't any question in my mind when I saw her though. A mix of Spanish and Asian, and a little African. Goddam! She looked like a woman from everywhere. One of the wildest and prettiest things I'd ever seen anywhere. She knew how to get what she wanted too. She was pushy enough to grab me, instead of waiting for someone else to get me. It was like I was in some movie. She dragged me away, through the girls who were still trying to get my buddy Pete to pick, and pulled me across the patio to a table.

I think Pete felt all of them first. Then, when he made up his mind he and his girl came and sat with us."

Tommy was getting wrapped up in his story. And Nate was entranced, listening. He'd stopped eating.

"Now, down there, you have to work out a price between the girl and the management for what you want. I was never that big on wanting to stay in a whore house. When I sleep with a girl I like to sleep with her. A quick bang and get out of the room never made me feel that great. I like to wrap my arms around her and have her wrap her arms around me. I wanted her to sleep with me all night. I didn't give a shit what it cost. Anyhow. She kept having to go back and forth to the boss. They had to know where I was staying and all of that, so she lied and told them this big fancy hotel down on the outskirts of town. Las Brisas. Lucky, I dressed kind of good that night. I don't know whether the boss could tell or not, but he let her go. Shit. I think it cost me a hundred forty bucks. It was a lot of money. But I didn't give a damn. I paid it. She changed her clothes and got back out so fast that I knew she really wanted to go.

She was feisty too. I teased her about something in the cab and she threatened to burn my leg with a cigarette. I liked her right off the bat."

Tommy stopped for a moment. He shook his head. Nate started drifting back down from the cloud of dreams he had been on. "So? Did you go back to your hotel? What happened?"

"Yeah. We went back to my hotel. We spent the night there."

Nate was hanging in the air, dangling from the thread of the story. Tommy didn't seem to want to finish it. Nate was too lost in the dream to realize that. "Well, what happened?"

"She spent the night."

"Is that all. She just spent the night?"

"Well, you know what I mean. We did what you do."

"Jesus! I was getting all set up for a big ending, the way you were talking. You at least knew her name?"

"Yeah." Tommy began to act almost indignant, like Nate was digging into his secret past without any authorization.

"Well, what was it?"

"Her name was Dolores."

"Dolores. That's a pretty name."

"Yeah."

"That means sad, right? Latin, from going to church with my grand-mother," Tommy turned from Nate. In his chest was a fresh fire. He swallowed. Everything was fuzzy. He shifted in his seat. "I have to go back to my room." Tommy really wanted to get up right away, but he'd been in the same position too long, and was cramped up in it. He grabbed at the back of the chair, trying to get a hold on it. Nate got up to help. Tommy tried to wave him off and lost control. He started to tip over.

Nate jumped up, holding out his arms to help. He was reluctant to grab at Tommy, not knowing what might help, and what might make it worse. "Let me help you Tommy?

"Nah. I've got it. I can do it!"

Tommy was acting peeved, but Nate didn't understand why. It didn't stop him from keeping his hands out to catch him, just in case.

It took all of Tommy's energy to push himself up. He didn't want this burning in his chest, or the pain in his back anymore. He was suddenly terribly tired. He only wanted to sleep until all the pains were gone.

Nate wished he knew exactly how to help. He put both hands around the top of Tommy's right arm.

"I don't need help. I can make it by myself."

"Yeah. Okay. I guess I was just hoping to hear more of the story. I was getting interested."

"There isn't any more goddam story. That was all there was to it. After that we did it. You're not the kind of guy who wants to hear how other people did it, are you?"

For a moment Nate was confused. He didn't know why he wanted to hear more of the story. Maybe he was one of those guys who likes to hear how other people do it. "I don't know. I just wanted to know what happened. I thought it was going to keep going."

"Well that's all of it. I don't have any more."

"Okay. Okay! I don't want to drag it out of you."

Tommy tried to walk as if no one was with him, and as if he didn't need anyone with him. All he wanted was to be back in his room, in bed. Nate followed Tommy's slow steps to the door. The old fart really wasn't in any shape to be out by himself. Nate wished he'd let him help him to his hotel room.

■ ■ ■

The taxi bumped out of the driveway. Dolores scooted over on the seat. She took his upper arm in her small, cool hands, like she had on the patio, and watched out the front of the cab, like she was looking out the window into the future. She turned back to Tommy and poked him in the side with her finger. There was an Asian little-girl playfulness that sparked in her eyes. Tommy wasn't sure why he thought it was Asian. Maybe Singapore. It just reminded him of that. His Spanish wasn't real good; he only knew a few words. He was embarrassed to try them and get them all fucked up. He didn't want to be in the cab. He wanted to be in the hotel room already, where he could speak a language that was the same all over the world. "Around the world". He smiled at his own private joke. Dolores grabbed his lips in her fingers when he smiled to himself. He pulled her fingers down, but held onto her hand. She was smiling at him, so he leaned over and pushed his lips against hers. Sometimes, when you kiss a woman, her lips are tightened up and formal. It's a sign of affection, but they have other things on their mind. They're saying, 'don't try to kiss me too long'. There are all kinds of kisses. This one was special. It was crazy really. He didn't understand it at all. Maybe she just knew what she was doing. Maybe she had been trained from the time she was little to do this. Tommy didn't know. Her lips melted into Tommy's like the hot Acapulco night had turned her to soft butter. She became so soft and pliant he couldn't tell what was her and what was his own imagination. Tommy breathed deep through his nose. Her perfume made gardenias bloom in his lungs. The taxi could have flown off the side of the hill out toward the stars and Tommy wouldn't have cared or known the difference. He became a dream.

thirteen

Martin stopped at Twenty Second Street, half-cocked at the curb, watching the stream of cars. He slapped the pole impatiently with his stick. The light finally switched, and pulled the cars up short, holding them impatiently back. Martin lumbered into the crosswalk, bent over slightly, unconcerned.

In the middle lane, a Ferrari rolled forward, and then back in line twice as he approached. Then it squeezed quickly forward again and sat over the line. With little thought, Martin grabbed the stubbed-up bottom of his cane in his left hand and cracked it on the hood of the red car. The Ferrari bucked angrily as the driver tried to shut it off. Martin swung his stick back down and kept lumbering. The light changed to yellow. A teenage boy leapt up out of the car, anger twisting his powerless face all into O's.

"Hey, fucking Geronimo Asshole! Come on back! I'll break your other fucking goat leg!"

Martin laughed noiselessly. He was no goat. He'd never be skittish. Without breaking a step, he reached his dark, meaty hand around, and flipped a soaring bird at the kid's nose. The screech of an eagle whirled around Martin's head as the red car shot away on the crowded street. Martin lumbered the rest of the way to the other curb, always moving ahead. Never deterred. On the other sidewalk, he headed straight for the door of El Charro Amigo.

Martin went straight to the boy who was always behind the counter on weekends, and ordered a beef burrito and a Tecaté with lemon.

The tabletops in El Charro are covered with cutout photographs of famous people, most of them movie stars or singers. Martin's favorite table was the movie star women. He headed straight there with his beer, and plopped in the chair, facing the back of the restaurant. A group of guys back there kept getting louder by the minute. They looked like jerks from a soccer team, in their silly-ass shorts and high socks. Fuck 'em. Fuck 'em all with a soccer ball. He laughed to himself, and turned his attention to his favorite tabletop.

His favorite picture on the tabletop was Jane Fonda, dressed in skimpy Neanderthal animal skins. But no Neanderthals ever cut their skins like Jane's, just right to show off what she had to offer. Martin would have eaten her if she walked in right now. He was as hungry for her as he was for the burrito he had coming. He grabbed the can of cold Tecaté, and pushed the wedge of lemon off the top. It bounced and fell on its wet side. Bright beads of lemon juice glistened on some other movie starlet's lips.

Looking over the top of his beer can as he took a slug, Martin noticed a young girl now leaning on the customer side of the back counter. She was reading an order to the boy. She was probably seventeen. Her breasts mashed against the counter top. Martin caressed her fancy jean butt with his eyes. She smiled at the boy, at some joke he had just told. Martin didn't give a shit about them. The boy glanced at Martin, then said something quietly to the girl. She peeked sideways and stood up, away from the counter. Her smile was gone. Her butt straightened. She gave the order again. Martin's eager lips were the counter edge. Her shirt was red and white striped. He could see the outline of her bra, pulling at her back.

The regular woman came out from behind the counter, bringing Martin his burrito. When she stepped right into his line of vision, his attention turned reluctantly.

Martin shook his heavy head. Her face was roundly fleshy, centered by a large nose. Her body had gone to that extra-fleshy state so many did after marriage. She was probably about twenty-five. She lifted his resting beer can, to test it. "Would you like something else?"

Martin bent to look around her. The young girl had now moved behind the counter to talk to the boy while he cooked. The other woman turned and went back and joined them. Martin knew her, and he knew the boy because their family owned the place. But the young girl was damn tasty-looking! He hadn't ever seen her before. He'd trade his burrito for her. He'd trade Jane for her. Jane was getting up there, but she had been really tasty-looking too. In the picture, her legs were long and dark. Her right arm held her dry, rough-blown hair out behind her head, like her whole body was a cave-village, dirt-floor, offering. Kind of a hard choice. But she was only a picture. Who knew what she was really like? Probably stuck-up as hell. Most movie assholes were stuck-up.

They were making a movie once in a bar down on Valencia. Martin wanted to hang around to see who was in it. Fucking cops kept running him off. One pig son of a bitch started to go for his nightstick on Martin. Hey! He had as much fucking right to be on the street as some asshole movie star! It was a fucking free country. The land had belonged to him first anyway. These fuckers were ALL trespassing. Fuck them! Martin would have loved it if the fucker had just put a bump on his head. He could have sued for police brutality. Shit!! Martin WANTED him to pull the thing out and use it. He'd be on easy street right now. It would be easy living. Martin reached with the plastic spoon and dipped hot sauce on his burrito. It was free. What the hell. He liked it. He took a swig of his beer. He looked back up. The girl had come out from behind the counter, carrying plates of food to the laughing-ass soccer jokers in the back of the room. Martin watched her young butt wiggle. He was ready for heaven. One of the soccer punks glared Martin's way.

Fuck you piss-head! No sissy Latino could tell him what to look at. Her titties hung tight in that striped shirt. She leaned her joy mound against the end of their table. Martin wanted to be a table. She turned to come back as he was draining the last of his beer. He lowered the can so it wouldn't block his vision. She glanced at him, then pulled herself quickly behind the counter. She stood near the boy, saying something. He didn't turn Martin's way. What the fuck. She was just a little girl. Nobody really gave a shit. Right? Everything was for a price. Like a burrito and a beer. Everything had a price. There wasn't anything that couldn't be bought. It was a fucking joke, all this shit about girls... It was just shit... It was all the same. No matter how you did it. Mountain lions grabbed them by the back of the neck so they couldn't get away. Porcupines couldn't do that though. Martin laughed. He looked to see if there was anything left to eat. He took a spoonful of the hot sauce and put it in his mouth. He dropped the spoon back in the sauce and a red drop splashed out into one of Paul Newman's bright eyes. The only man on this whole table of women. He'd probably had his share of them. No shit!

Martin didn't want to be fucking Paul Newman, though. Pansy-ass honkie. He didn't want any more hot sauce. What the fuck, he paid for it though. He paid for everything. Fuck them. Who really cared? He was ready to pay for anything. Martin reached down to his pocket and felt the hill of change. He probably had twenty-five dollars in all of his different pockets. He grabbed his cane, getting up and leaving the check on the table. He started toward the back of the restaurant as if heading to the bathroom. The girl, with more plates in her hands, stopped at the counter opening, waiting for him to pass. Martin stopped just next to her. Fuck them. He could pay for what he wanted. After stalling, confused for a moment, she started in front of him. Martin reached out to put his hand on her arm. "Wait a minute." She stopped, balancing the plates. She turned her head quickly to look back over her shoulder at the boy, who was busy filling cokes from the fountain. Martin almost whispered. "No. Just wait a minute." He leaned down close to her face and spoke even more quietly. "I don't want anybody else to hear...." Her big, dark, calf eyes widened, then began to dart around. "Would you do me a favor please?" She looked at Martin, confused. "Would you please sit on my face?" She didn't seem to understand him at all. She tried to pull away gently, careful of the plates. He lightly grabbed her arm. "No. You don't understand. I just want you to sit on my face. That's all." The boy turned from the coke machine. Martin kept on. "You don't understand. I just want you to sit on my face." Martin smiled. "That's all." She glanced back toward the soccer players. The one who had been watching Martin got out of his chair. The others followed him with their eyes. Martin felt like laughing. He lifted his hand with the cane in it and put his finger on his nose. "You know. Just sit on my face. Right here. That's all."

The cook reached around and took one of the girl's plates out of her hand and pulled on her to try to get her back behind the counter.

Martin wouldn't let go.

The boy lifted his right arm, picking up a spatula. "Let go of her, just this moment," he blurted in a thick accent.

Martin almost laughed.

The soccer player reached carefully around the girl for Martin. "Get your hand off her!"

He was short and stocky. He smelled of sweat. The grip of his fist on Martin's arm was stiff and tight. Martin laughed in his face. "You don't understand. I just want her to sit on my face. That's all." Martin put his finger to his nose again. "Right here." He started to drop himself to the floor, pulling still on her thin arm. "I just want her to sit on my face."

The soccer kid grabbed up higher, by Martin's shoulder. The older girl moved nearer Martin and reached across the counter, trying to reach him with her fist. She hollered. "Let her go! Get out of here!"

The little girl yanked at her arm. He wanted to hold it tighter but didn't. The boy pulled her behind the counter and jumped in front of Martin, holding the spatula above his head. Martin laughed. The boy reached to the back counter, without turning his eyes, and grabbed up a wooden tortilla press. With a clear field, the soccer player grabbed Martin by both arms and shoved him hard, toward the front of the restaurant. Martin was angry now. He stopped laughing. He tried to raise his walking stick. The older girl screeched again. "Get out of here!!" Martin tried to stop himself. He stumbled backwards, trying to grab something with his hands. "You don't understand. I only wanted her to sit on my face." That got him laughing again. At the cash register, Martin dug his left foot in to a halt. The older woman ran forward and grabbed the ticket spike from the counter, tickets fluttering on it. She pushed it toward him, her eyes now larger than her nose, threatening to puncture his.

"Get out of here. Pig!!" The soccer player twisted Martin and kicked him in the ass. Martin tried to turn back, but was shoved from behind, much too hard. He stumbled, almost falling into a quiet old couple he hadn't seen in there. They cringed from him in their booth. Martin was rammed violently again, past them. It took all of his effort just to stay on his feet. At the door he felt a sneaker foot against his ass. He had to laugh out loud, stumbling through the door.

Outside, under their low overhang, Martin leaned back, as close to having his head inside as he could get, almost in the punk soccer kid's face. "I just wanted her to sit right here!" He lifted the cane to his nose again. "Right here!!" He laughed again, as loud as he could.

fourteen

Tommy nearly stumbled off the curb at Wiese Alley, his feet barely shuffling. Nate wanted to keep an eye where they walked, but it was hard to hold his mind to it. He kept wanting to look up and around. At the opposite curb he forced himself to pay careful attention. A loud low-rider heading toward Mission pulled to a stop. Salsa music blared out the open windows of the car. The speakers had been blown long ago, but that didn't stop him from playing it as loud as it went. The noise was ugly, but the beat was unmistakable. Tommy didn't seem to notice.

Nate was about to turn his attention back to Tommy when a bus pulled up behind the low-rider. The bus brakes squealed out another ugly song. Nate wished he could turn his ears the way he could turn his eyes. He glimpsed something on the bus, halfway down its length, something almost orange and deep green. Nate's chest skipped a breath. When the bus pulled up further, he was certain. He watched her. She turned, as if expectant for something, to look out the other side of the bus. Tommy bobbed and pulled at Nate's hands. Nate grabbed tighter. He had to turn back. He whipped his right hand around to grab Tommy's other side. Tommy let out a groan.

"Goddam. Fuck. That hurts!"

"I know. I'm sorry, Tom. I had to grab you to keep you from falling."

"Jesus! Cocksucker! Call me Tommy, will ya?"

Nate was sure Tommy was angry with him. But he couldn't have let the old fart go. He wondered if people thought they were just a couple of drunks stumbling through a Sunday binge.

When they were at the doors of the hotel, Nate heard a blast of compressed air as the electric bus released its brakes and took off quietly. His ears tried to leave with it.

fifteen

With every block they moved, the bus jerking across Sixteenth, Henrietta felt her world grow smaller, dimmer. Her temporary respite at Soon Lee had been nothing more.

Getting out just on the other side of South Van Ness, Henrietta raised her eyes to the front of the hotel, to her room on the third floor. Air pulled the curtain out of the window frame. For a sliver of a moment she thought something moved in her room, through the curtain parting. Had she left the window open? She couldn't remember. Henrietta headed toward the hotel. There was nowhere else to go, and she didn't have any more money on her.

She passed a man in the crosswalk. He had deep lines in his face that ran up from his mouth to his cheeks. And lines too, carving his cheeks and his chin. His eyes were deep in his head, under thick wiry brows. In the center of his forehead was a dark vertical wrinkle. It must have been from thinking. His mottled gray-brown hair fell straight down out of a leather cap. She wondered what he thought so much about. She wondered if his hands were as strong as they looked. They were well-used, like a builder's.

Just before the other curb, Henrietta angled toward the hotel. On either side of South Van Ness now, they were moving parallel. She watched him out of the edge of her eye. She couldn't see if he was watching her. At the front of the hotel, she stopped. If they had been on a street in a painting, then somewhere, in the distance, they would have converged, out there at the point of perspective. She thought about walking on. But there were no converging lines in her life. There never really had been. Things just ran on and on and on.

Henrietta stepped into the hotel and forced her mind to close down. She tried not to look as she passed the clerk's window. Too many times he had hinted to her about getting a reduced rate on her room. She always pretended she didn't understand. His dense glasses were almost as thick as the bullet-proof window of his cubicle. She tried not to look out into the lobby either, at its spread-out plastic couches, peopled with the afternoon-loungers who would watch her go by, pointing at her and making comments to each other.

Riding in the elevator, her eyes didn't want to focus. She stared at graffiti scratched in the door paint. She had no idea what it said. She was back looking out South Van Ness Street, converging out near the base of Bernal Hill, and she was walking toward that convergence, while a man across the street moved toward the same convergence. But she had no idea who he was, or even what he looked like.

When the doors slumped open, Henrietta stepped out, still not really seeing where she was. As she moved down the dingy red carpet toward her room, she controlled a growing sense of trepidation. The walls of the hall became real to her. It was merely her dislike for this place. She pulled the key from her bag. Grandma's letter stuck to her damp hand as she tried to untangle it from the keys. She stuffed it back in the purse the way you do when you aren't sure how you feel about something; treating it carelessly, waiting for it to find its own importance. She grabbed the door knob with her left hand. It turned without using the key. Something in her heart jumped suddenly, leaving a buzzing in her chest and throat. She pushed it quietly. Suction from the window almost yanked it from her hand. She turned sharply, to look down the hall. A tall man near the other end, who looked to have a nearly shaved head and a big nose, closed a room door behind him. He was wearing a big, bulging overcoat. Why was he wearing an overcoat in October? He stopped to gaze at Henrietta. Something moved quickly across his face. She didn't recognize him. He turned crisply. His long coat moved slowly, weighted. He headed into the stairwell. Henrietta turned her attention back to the room. The door was all the way open and her curtains fluttered out the window. Everything was the same as she always left it, except the door and window. She crossed to the open window. Between the snapping curtains, her eyes scanned the opposite sidewalk. No one was out there but people getting gas. She left the window open, relishing the cool freedom of the air. She threw her purse on the bed, then studied the way the pillow was under the covers. She hadn't made the bed like that. It was always perfectly tucked under when she left the room. Something in her heart thumped wrong. Henrietta spun around in the room. The door to the closet was a little open. The lampshade on the dresser hung crooked on the lamp. Was she really that far from herself that she left things like this? Quickly, she opened the third drawer in her dresser. She grabbed under the clothes. Her little purse wasn't there. She swept her hands through the drawer again, pushing under the hose and the socks and the underwear. She took the things out of the drawer. She could be missing it. She threw each piece behind her on the bed, making sure to squeeze it first. It wasn't there. She pushed herself up and ran to the door. Her throat constricted. Out in the hall now, the word 'THIEF' bounced in her head. THIEF! She wasn't sure she hadn't yelled it. Henrietta grabbed the front edge of the door as she stomped back into the room. She slammed it! Tromping to the dresser she crammed the drawer back in and yanked out the other ones, one by one. The gold bracelet was gone too. The one that Grandma had given her. The tears crowding her eyes weren't like other tears she had felt before. They were sharp stones trying to squeeze from under her burning lids. Her chest, her legs and her arms grew thick and stiff.

"Goddam motherfucking sonsabitches." She may as well have muffled it into her mattress. Her voice had no power in the room. She began again. "Goddam...." She stopped. Then taking the three steps to the window, she pushed the curtains out, tangling her hands. The guy in the bulging overcoat was hurrying on the sidewalk. "Goddam fucking sonsabitches!"

He turned his head. Their eyes met immediately. His face was a controlled blank. He pulled his vulture head down quickly and ducked under a small tree to a car. She heard the door slam. It came up from the street muffled. The car started off quietly, and pulled out to make a U-turn to head downtown. It lumbered away, big and brown, rocking back and forth, unconcerned.

Henrietta pulled her head into the room. Her socks and underwear were on the bed and floor, all twisted up. She wanted to fall in the jumble on the bed, in all those soft things, and roll in them.

That's what she used to want to do when she was little; pull Grandma's cool, silky things out of the drawer and spread them on the bed to comfort in them. She'd never done it.

Henrietta stood. She almost stomped her foot. Goddammit! She had to stop and think.

sixteen

Glancing around the lobby of Tommy's hotel, Nate realized, even small it must have been pretty nice at one time. The openness of what must have been a long front desk had been blocked-off by an ugly, scuffed-up, white wall. Only a small clerk's window now peeked out of it, to keep a close eye on whoever came and went. There was still a fancy gate on the elevator, and up above them, a fancy-railed balcony overlooking the lobby.

"Hey. Where are you going there? You must check in at the desk clerk." The voice had the slight, sing-song, elegance of an Indian accent. Nate glanced back toward the opening in the wall. There was a small man with dark skin, poking his white-turbaned head through the window. His face protruded in the middle, sweeping back at the forehead and in at the chin, thin, like a rat's.

"Where are you going? You cannot merely enter this hotel. You must register, and if you are visiting someone you must leave your name at the desk clerk. I must not let you wander this hotel at will."

Tommy turned his head to the clerk. "He's helping me to my room."

"I see. You haven't been drinking? You know we do not desire drunks."

Nate piped up, slightly angry. "He's been hurt. He lives here. I'm just helping him to his room."

The clerk hesitated, as if he needed to assess the type of damage Tommy had sustained. After a quiet, scrutinizing moment he waved his hand dismissedly. "You go up, then."

Tommy didn't have the energy to react.

Nate was angry. He yanked the elevator gate open. Nate waited for Tommy to move inside and held onto the side rail while Nate slid the brass-plated gate behind them.

"Fourth floor. Four eighteen."

"Okay Tom. Got it. Hold tight for takeoff."

"And Call me Tommy, will ya?"

Nate looked at him and nodded assent, "Sure," as the elevator lurched upward. Tommy grabbed the handrail tighter. Nate reached out, ready, but didn't touch Tommy, who had his eyes closed.

The machine lurched to a stop, and Tommy managed to keep his knees from buckling. When Nate opened the door, the car had stopped two inches below Tommy's floor. Nate took hold of Tommy's arm again. "Watch out here."

"It does that every time. Fucking Indians. They don't give a shit. They own all the hotels, so you can't make them do anything."

Nate was thoughtful. "I don't think they own the one I live in. The Mission."

"I'm not surprised. It's in too good a shape for them. They only buy run-down ones, so they can keep the heat off, and get away without hot water.

Nate watched the door numbers while they moved slowly down the linoleum corridor. "The goddam Mission is no picnic park either, let me tell you, Tommy."

Tommy reached into his pocket and felt for his key. "Oh shit!"

"What's the matter?"

Tommy pulled his other arm out of Nate's grasp, and felt in that pocket. "Good. I thought I lost my goddam key. And these assholes charge five dollars for a new one."

Tommy handed the key to Nate. He worked it into the old brass lock in the scarred wooden door. Light flooded into the hall as the door opened. Tommy's old-style room was a lot larger than Nate's.

Tommy's room was at the front corner of the building, with windows on two sides. The paint was peeling off the walls in the corner. Probably old mortar joints breaking down, Nate thought. He could see out the one window to the towers on Twin Peaks. The other looked across Sixteenth Street, at the bank and the city parking lot. It wasn't a bad room. Tommy kept the place fairly neat. Everything seemed to be where it should be. The bed was all rumpled though. "You want me to turn down the bed for you?"

"I'm not an old woman. I appreciate you helping me get to my room, but I can handle it from here." Tommy had the sudden fear that maybe Nate could be planning to come back later and rob him. It had happened before to other old farts. Some guys liked to roll old men. It was easy. "I can take it from here. I don't need any more help."

"Are you sure? Can't I help you get into bed or something?"

"No. I can do that myself. I told you, I'm not an old woman."

Tommy shuffled to the bed and let himself down on the edge. He didn't look very comfortable to Nate.

Tommy reached toward the pillow, resting his hand on the cover, ready to pull it back. "I'll be all right. I keep a gun under my pillow. Nobody can bother me."

"I wasn't talking about that. I meant just some help getting set up. Because of your back. That was all."

Tommy kept his hand on the pillow, looking at Nate curiously, almost as if he didn't trust him. Nate shrugged his shoulders. "If there's anything you want help with, I'm at the Mission Hotel. You can call and leave a message. Like if you want help getting to the doctor or something. Or you want some food picked up."

Tommy kept his hand on the cover, near the pillow. He didn't even know if he had the strength to pull the spread back. If Nate wanted to hurt him, it wouldn't be any trouble. He didn't keep any fucking gun under his pillow. He'd never liked guns.

Tommy only wanted to lie down. He didn't want to have to worry about being robbed. He didn't have anything worth shit anyway.

Nate sighed. "I'll see you later Tommy. I hope you feel better." Tommy looked up with no expression on his face. Nate shrugged and pulled the door quietly to behind him.

Tommy let his hand slide from the pillow. He sighed, alone now. He couldn't fall back onto the mattress. He had to muster the energy to get into the bed the right way. He pushed his shoes off, one foot helping the other. He didn't want to wrestle with his pants now. "Goddammit!" Blowing a gust of air from his lungs he pushed up slowly from the bed and began to unbuckle his heavy belt.

seventeen

Nate flowed effortlessly with the stream of street noise. Cars rolled by, slow, with loud salsa chunking from their open windows. Horns blared impatiently at intersections. Off toward Potrero Hill, a siren screamed, probably rushing to General. A couple of Latinos were yelling back and forth across the street to each other. One was near Nate, bouncing on the corner; the other over by the mouth of the BART entrance, waving. As Nate crossed Mission, a train whooshed to a stop underneath the street. The tunnel pressure blew out of the giant grate about ten feet away. Too bad there were no giggling Spanish girls standing over them in skirts. A 22 bus pulled into the curb on Sixteenth. The BART plaza was buzzing with people. Nate kept walking, calmly, deliberately, through it all.

By Capp Street, things were quieter, but the action on Mission still rattled in his ears. Nate didn't mind. He began to walk a little faster toward the hotel. He didn't know why. He had no reason to feel optimistic or energetic.

Nate angled off the sidewalk and out into Sixteenth to cross, just before South Van Ness. He stopped in the middle of the street for a station wagon full of teenage baseball players heading across Sixteenth toward Potrero. They looked All-American, like the kids he used to see in Carmel, or back when he lived in Memphis. They were more fresh-faced than the kids he usually saw in the Mission; just teenagers, growing up the way teenagers on TV did. Nate watched as their heavy car slowed and dipped through the intersection; boys in the back slapping each other with their hats, laughing as the car moved heavily away from him.

Across South Van Ness, the gas station was busy, but no noise floated over to him. Two teenage girls stepped out of the hotel and came toward him. He had never seen them before. One was starting to plump. She had dark, Hispanic hair. She wore a lot of make-up. The other girl was Hispanic too, but her hair was an odd color that feinted in several directions; toward red and brown and blonde. Her face was soft, fleshy and full. She had full lips and cheeks and a round, gracious chest. Her white blouse was all ruffles, emphasizing her breasts. They swayed past him. As his head turned to follow, he bowed a little toward the ground. His sweeping eye caught a golden flash. Torn between curiosity and lust, Nate swung his head back to where he thought he saw the spot of light, under a tree at the edge of the sidewalk. He impulsively twisted back to watch the blonde girl disappear around the corner. Then he turned back and knelt toward the sidewalk. In the dirt and trash at the tree's base, a golden bracelet was strung out, half in the shade of a hamburger wrapping. Nate lifted it by the clasp end. It was heavier than he had thought. He looked both ways down the sidewalk, then back at the bracelet. It was made of domed, interlocking, H-shaped links. He slinked it into his other hand and glanced around again. A black man had come around the corner. Nate stood up. He wondered if the bracelet could be real gold. He wadded it tightly in his hand and hurried toward the hotel. As the fast-moving black man neared, Nate tensed. He jumped across the man's path and up to the hotel entrance.

Inside, a woman's voice was echoing in that cheap hotel lobby way. "You BETTER do something!" Nate's skin jumped. His nerves were screeching all of a sudden. He glanced back to be certain the black man had passed on, then peered again into the lobby. His heart jumped. The red-haired girl was in a fit over something with the clerk. She looked mad enough to smash her fist against the bullet-proof window. Nate approached slowly. He saw that her face was contorted, from crying as much as from anger. Her hair hung thick and long on her back, in heavy orange-red strands.

Nate remembered seaweed on a lonely Carmel beach at sundown. Waves washed at it, red, as it looped in and tugged out. A wave ran in, splashing, wrapping the red seaweed around his legs. His heart choked with panic. He almost yelled, but then the wave suddenly slowed and the seaweed unwrapped from his leg and floated back out on the receding tide. Nate watched it slide off the back of the next wave, and then ride out there. He wanted to splash out and dive into all the seaweed. He wanted it to grab him by the ankles and hold him by his wrists, wrapping around his naked neck.

Nate moved no closer to the redheaded woman. He heard the soft voice of the clerk behind the bullet-proof glass.

"Calm down. I can't do anything. Why don't you go file a police report?"

"You saw him didn't you? Will you at least tell them what he looked like?" She was pleading now, exasperated.

"Sorry. I didn't see anybody who wasn't supposed to be here. What did this so-called thief take?"

Benny's tone was agitating her more. She seemed about to explode, and then her voice suddenly became pathetic. "He took all my money...."

Benny wasn't moved. "Don't you keep any in the bank?"

"No. I told you, he took all the money I had. Except for a little bit I had in my purse with me."

"You know, your rent is due tomorrow."

"I know that!" She must have been on the verge of calling him some damn good name, but then she held back. "It probably wouldn't matter to you that he took my grandmother's antique gold bracelet too."

Nate's hand closed tightly in his pocket. He could feel the edges of the gold links angled into his palm. The tops of the links were rounded and comforting.

"It might matter to the police. Why don't you file a report, like I said? But if you don't have any money you might want to start figuring out how you're going to pay rent tomorrow."

"What's..?" Nate had to clear his throat. "What's the bracelet like?"

She snapped around to him. For a moment, the conflicting tides of her wrath and her pleading washed over him. Her face softened to a suspicious curiosity. "Why?"

Nate twisted the fist in his pocket as he moved closer to her. He stopped about four or so feet away. Her female attention made him nervous, no matter what its elements were. "I was just wondering." He added. Her face changed again.

Maybe he was just another one of those weird people who seemed to be everywhere now. What was he doing near her again? She heard herself speaking to him anyway, throwing it off. "It was a gold link bracelet that my grandmother gave me."

"I just meant what did it look like?" Nate held the bracelet firmly in his pocket. He was half-leaning toward the wall of the desk clerk's cubicle. She put her right hand to her forehead, looking a little impatient with his question. Then she dropped it down to her left wrist, holding that for a moment.

"It was gold, and had links that were hooked together." She seemed to know how silly that description was. "And they were shaped like this." Her hand in the air, she tried to trace a shape. She knew quickly that that didn't work either. She gazed into his face, wanting to know what he was about, what he wanted. His hair was darker than hers, almost brown, but he'd be called a red-head too. She had never been attracted to red-heads. She wasn't attracted to him either. He just wasn't her type. She kept looking into his eyes. They were blue. The right one had a speck of another color in the corner of it, on the outside of the iris. It looked green. Her eyes were green. She had never known anyone with a two-tone eye before. She had known people with two different-colored eyes before. What the hell was she thinking? She didn't know him. She didn't want to know anything about him. She tried to keep the picture of his penis dangling in his open robe out of her head. His pubic hair, what she had seen of it, was a golden red. She didn't want to think about it. She glimpsed down to his jeans involuntarily, quickly passing his crotch, trying to control herself. He had a scrape on his well-worn knee. It looked like he had fallen on the sidewalk. She thought of a little kid. That's what his eye reminded her of. It was the kind of trick eye that a little kid might like to see in his teasing grandfather's face. He kept twisting his right hand in his pocket. He seemed to be uncomfortable. She wanted to smile to herself. The expression on his face hadn't changed. He seemed to be waiting for her to describe the bracelet completely. Why? She had to think a little more.

Nate watched her as she looked down, trying to remember. She lifted her eyes back to his face, then raised her hands in front of her. She slid her thumbs and first fingers together. Her hands were loose fists under the open fingers. It looked a bit like a staggered 'H' to Nate. He stopped twisting his hand in his pocket. He pulled his fist out and held it up to her, opening it. "Was it like this?" She dropped her eyes to his hand.

As her eyes widened, Nate felt his own pull open. She stepped closer and bent down toward his hand. He was looking into her hair. She was a true redhead. Her hair had the colors of sun; every sun that had ever been; red, or orange, or yellow, even almost white.

"That's the bracelet! Where did you get it?!'

She seemed reluctant to touch it in his palm, as if she had lost ownership of it. He pushed his hand to her a little. She lifted the bracelet by one end, and then brought her eyes to his face. The tears were there again, but different, bigger, shining.

"How do I know you two didn't stage this whole thing, trying to figure some way to keep from her having to pay the rent?"

Henrietta and Nate turned toward the clerk's voice. Henrietta's eyes narrowed. Her forehead wrinkled. Nate scanned Benny's fat, weak face. His hair was black, combed back with grease. His face was round, jowly from eating too much; his way of storing what little wealth he could cadge or hoard. Benny's thick glasses pushed into his fat cheeks. His eyes bulged behind the distorting lenses. There was nothing Nate could say to him. He turned, disgusted, back to the girl.

Henrietta threw a quick glare of contempt through the window. For a fleeting moment she wondered sharply how this guy happened to be here, right now, with her bracelet. She peeked into his eye for a quick moment. That piece of green in the corner of the right iris seemed to be some childish proof he couldn't have been in on a plan to do this to her.

Her face changed almost as she was looking at him. He was glad he had found the bracelet for her. He was glad she had it back.

"I don't have any money. They took that too, or I would give you something. I can't tell you how important this bracelet is to me. I wish I could do something."

His neck began to itch. His boot was bothering his foot. Nate stared at the floor. He wanted out of the lobby.

"You two can't fool me."

They swung back to the clerk as if controlled by the same set of puppet strings.

"Just remember your rent is due tomorrow. If you want to talk about it, I'll be here until ten tonight. After that I'm going to be off, and it'll be too late."

Henrietta stood for a moment. She imagined the clerk coming into her room.

Nate felt suddenly left out. He started to go around the girl.

She spoke up quickly, stopping him. "I wish I knew your name so I could at least thank you properly."

Her voice had a softness that held him there. Her face seemed sincere, but distressed, as if she were losing something else now. "It's Nathan. I... I mean Nate."

"I really want to thank you, Nathan."

"It wasn't anything. I just found it outside under a tree."

She grabbed at this thread. "Where? Could you show me?"

"Yeah. It was under a tree, next to the curb."

Her face lit up. "I knew it. I saw the guy who stole it get into a brown car right by that tree, I knew he was the one. Maybe now they'll believe me."

"I believe you."

Henrietta threw a sharp glance over her shoulder and narrowed her eyes again at the clerk's cage.

"Don't pay any attention to him. Benny can't help it he's just an asshole."

Henrietta leaned toward Nate like she was sharing a confidence. "That's exactly how I would put it."

Nate shrugged his right shoulder, embarrassed. "He really is."

"I know. I won't even tell you all the things...."

"Don't worry, I'd believe it."

She put her hand on his wrist, below his rolled-up sleeve. The hairs tickled her palm. It had been a long time since she had held a man's arm. She liked it. The bones weren't large, but he felt strong. "Would you help me if I called the police?" Her voice had a friendly plead to it. Not helpless, but needing help.

Nate focused on her eyes. "What would I be able to do?"

She held to his arm. He liked her hand there. He could almost feel her breath as she spoke. "You could tell them where you found the bracelet. Then they would at least know that part. You didn't see the car, did you? It was a big brown one. Kind of old. With two guys in it?"

"No. I must have been too late."

"It was about a half hour ago. But I had to ask anyway. Would you help me if I call the police?"

Nate watched her mouth. The skin of her lips was a pale, bleached pink. It was a big mouth. There was one tiny freckle just a little off center of her lower lip. It was brown and made the pale flesh around it fascinating. There was fine blonde hair on her upper lip.

"I guess." He said. "Are you going to call them now?"

"I think I better. Will you wait for them with me?"

"Sure." They had unknowingly edged toward the doors, away from Benny's window. Nate glanced around the lobby, over toward the fireplace, as if wondering what he would do while waiting for the police.

"Please?"

She must have taken his search of the room as a sign of impatience. He tried to calm her immediately. "Nah, I was just wondering where you want to wait. Do you want to call them from here? Or do you want to go somewhere else to be away from him?" He bent his head back over his shoulder as he mentioned the clerk. Her lips were open. They again became the focus of his eyes.

"I don't care about him." She said. "I think we ought to just do it here. We have to wait here anyway."

"Okay." Nate stepped toward the little alcove by the front doors, where the phone and cigarette machine were kept. She followed.

There was a six by six inch window that looked out into the alcove from Benny's office, allowing him to keep an eye on what might be happening there. Nate immediately leaned with his hand spread out covering the little window, knowing Benny would want to watch them through it. When she dialed the number from the book, Nate began to feel like an eavesdropper himself. He didn't want to leave Benny free to spy on her, but he was uncomfortable, so close in that small space. He had to move, and slipped back around the wall to lean heavily against the lobby side. The RC machine in the alcove hummed cold. The couches down in the middle of the slightly sunken lobby were probably cold too, upholstered in plastic; in aquamarine, rose, burnt orange; colors like that. Nate looked toward the back hall, where daylight was still dropping down the stairwell, and then out to the street, where cars were sliding by at intervals, then back to the brick fireplace down in the middle of the lobby, gaping black and cold.

Nate's ears picked up words and phrases that slipped around the wall into the lobby. They were things he already knew; "Mission Hotel", and "gold bracelet". He heard her say something that sounded like "Henrietta Felix". Her name? Henrietta? Nate's unconscious eavesdropping made him begin to wonder what Benny was doing in that quiet lock-up of a room of his. He snuck down to the lobby window and peeked in.

Just like he had figured; Benny had the TV turned all the way down and was pressing up to the small pane trying to hear Henrietta.

Nate tiptoed back to the front doors and leaned quietly and quickly around the wall. Benny's form flashed in the small window as he ducked down. Concentrating on her phone call, Henrietta's back was to Nate. Her hair hung halfway down it. She was pushing it out of her face while she talked. Nate looked at her ass, bent over with the phone, her jeans tight blue. She had a fairly small waist. Her shirt crumpled softly there when she twisted. He couldn't see her breasts, but knew they were full. His spine tickled. He pulled quietly back around the corner, though he didn't want to. He rolled against the wall and stared down at his boots, thoughtful. They were scuffed, the smooth, dark, upper leather giving way to rough, paler brown. The heels were worn low. But he knew all that already. He looked at the scrape on the knee of his jeans. He crossed the right knee over his left to hide it. He felt silly. His neck began to itch again, alive. He glanced around the corner, only far enough to see the RC machine, and he almost began to read it; as if it was interesting. He wanted to look back at Henrietta but couldn't think of a good reason. He was warm in his flannel shirt. He pushed at his rolled-up sleeves.

<h1 style="text-align:center">eighteen</h1>

In the falling Sunday light, something like the hush of a high mountain canyon drops into Mission Street. The noisy cars thin to a pleasant few. The sidewalks are free. In the new cool there is a flow of excited energy under the skin. Those that are out feel it.

When he shook his laughing head, the weight of Martin's long hair whipped around his face. He felt like shrieking into the light air. A strand of his swinging hair stuck in Martin's lips. He shook his head to throw it out.

"Oh!" He heard a woman's small scream next to him.

Martin turned, unconcerned, toward the noise. A short, round, Mexican woman was clawing at her mouth, spitting, almost squealing.

On the other side of her was a small Mexican man, a skinny Chihuahua to her roly-poly piglet. He held her by the arm and peeked around her. She spun toward Martin with anger in her eyes. "Your filthy hair!"

The man leaned around her further, like a small dog with his eyes bugging out of his thin head. "Leave my wife alone!" He yapped and pulled her away from Martin.

Martin noticed he didn't step between them. He watched them move off, curious. He was ready to laugh.

Her voice squealed like a tiny, tortured pig back Martin's way. "He threw his hair into my face," she said, as if exhorting her husband to act. She turned away from Martin, still spitting down. "Pig!!"

"Keep yourself to yourself." The tiny dog-man snapped back Martin's way with his tiny teeth.

Martin laughed. He recognized the fear in their eyes.

The man pulled a handkerchief from his jacket pocket and offered it to his wife.

Martin was free and strong. "Wheeeeeoooooppp!!" He shook his head back and forth. His hair swung wildly, whipping around his head. He moved on, placing his cane quickly, moving his feet in a true rhythm.

The cool air that blew down with the evening fog slipped between the buildings, giving Martin the energy to move faster.

His sense of power and freedom matched his ideas of himself. He knew now what he could do. He knew how fast he could run, and he knew how little he needed to run. The ability to fly above his prey and enemies was not needed. He could move among them in the freedom of his strength. Martin angled, stepping into the street. He didn't look for cars or wait for clear lanes. What cars there were, stopped quietly as he crossed in front of them.

When he was a teenager Martin used to wish he had been born a dog. Then he wouldn't give a shit about anything. All he'd ever do was just fuck girl dogs; out in the desert, out in the hills, in the street, behind buildings, in the basements of houses, in the living rooms of houses. That's all he would ever do, fuck and eat.

Later though, he wished he was an eagle. He noticed that dogs went around with their noses in the dirt, sniffing for things, staying out of the way, cringing when you threatened them. As an eagle he would always look down on the land, on his food; on people. He would be strong and he would be free. There were other animals he had wanted to be along the way, like a buck deer. But for certain, Martin didn't want to be a dog, though he could still feel the drive for the automatic thrust of the pelvis.

Lately, just recently, he was starting to think maybe he really wanted to be a bear. A bear is powerful, large. A bear answers to no one and cringes from no one. A bear decides his own life, moving at the speed he chooses. Martin would move slowly. He was becoming constantly more aware of his power.

He didn't notice his lumbering reflection in the cafe window as he turned into Clarion Alley. He moved steadily forward, as if heading for his den. Halfway down the tight alley, he stopped and looked around him; down the way he was heading, and behind, where he had come from. He checked carefully. There was no one close, no one watching. There were only those who moved past the canyon opening. He ambled quietly further, almost as if he knew of some familiar opening. Just in front of a low doorway on the left, he stopped. Without hesitating, he stepped up and moved in, deliberately, slowly. At the back end was a closed door leading to small steps. Martin didn't touch the door. He stopped and stood. Quiet.

After a moment, he began to pull off his jacket in the low, cramped space. He wadded it at first, as if thinking what to do with it. But then he un-wadded it again and dropped it on the floor at his feet. The buttons clacked as they hit on the cement. Martin began to peel off his shirts. He wore four of them. The first he unbuttoned. The second he yanked off, popping all the buttons. The last two he fought over his head together. He let the shirts fall willy-nilly, collecting around his legs. Lifting his feet, one by one, kicking his twisted shirts off, he tugged at his oversized boots, leaning against the cold wood door behind him. The boots had become cracked and very flexible with constant wearing. He set them on the floor in front of him.

Standing for a moment, he almost seemed to think about something. As if it was one of those absent thoughts just before you go to sleep. He slowly dropped himself to the pile of clothes wadded under him. He released the heavy belt and the buckle thumped on the little wall next to him. Martin began to pull off both pairs of pants at the same time, wriggling, with his ass now bared to the cool night. He pushed the pants out onto the floor too.

As if he was now settled, Martin slumped down onto his clothes. Leaning on his elbow, he arranged them under him, squashing out the bone-disturbing lumps. He was ready for the freedom of sleep.

nineteen

He heard Henrietta hang up the phone. She came around the wall and Nate turned to her. Her features were round. Her freckles seemed to stand out more now, as if the lobby light had become more like a glow. He realized he already thought of her as having that name. Henrietta. She stood in front of him. Her breasts were large. He tried not to look only at them. He wanted to push himself up straight, uncrossing his legs, but remembered the tear in his pants.

"They're coming in a few minutes Nathan." Her face was earnest.

"Don't believe that. It'll take them an hour to get here. Even if they come." Benny's voice only dribbled from the shielded hole in his protective window. Even so, he must have held his mouth right up to it. Henrietta didn't even turn in the direction of the clerk's voice.

Nate thought about going down to Benny's window and daring him out of the room. Benny wasn't trying to get Nate's attention, though.

She blinked her eyes, but kept them on Nate's. "Would you like to move over there?" She pointed offhandedly to the lobby.

What Nate really thought was that Benny could keep a better eye on them out there, but he kept it to himself, and only said. "Sure. That's okay with me."

Henrietta started to move, anxious.

Nate leaned to peek into her face for a moment, looking for something. "We could go to my room and wait."

Her eyes suddenly swept across his face, guided by some sharp thought.

Before he could name her expression Nate recoiled. He stuttered. "Or we could...go up to your room...I just mean...to be out of here...away from him."

Henrietta looked sharply into his face for a moment. "I know what you mean. But I think we better wait down here." She moved her head toward Benny. "I bet he wouldn't tell the police where we are."

"The lobby is fine with me. I don't mind waiting here." Nate's words came out transparently over-quick to him.

They both fell quiet as they stepped into clear sight of Benny's window, and down into the lobby. Henrietta looked to Nate for direction. He gazed around responsibly, then pointed to a little corner by the front windows. There they could have a little bit of wall between themselves and Benny.

They both remained quiet, secretive, as they dropped to the rose-colored plastic couch, their backs to the South wall so they could watch the street and the doors. Nate immediately turned to look out at the street, and stared, not knowing what he was staring at, not even knowing what he was thinking. Soon, he would have to talk, and he had no idea what to say. As he watched two cars jockeying for position at the gas station he heard his own voice, detached, nervous. "What did this guy get?"

He had to turn to her.

She gazed around the lobby, everywhere but in Nate's direction. "Everything I had left. A hundred and fifty five dollars."

"Oh shit. You're kidding me?!"

"No I'm not." Her head dropped as if it couldn't hold the weight of the realization.

"What are you going to do?"

"I've got to get it back. That's all there is to do."

Nate had to work to keep his pessimistic opinion off his face. "Do you think the police can do that?"

"They have to. It's my only chance. I'm not kidding. When I say I don't have any more money, I mean it. I might have about three dollars in my purse, but that's it." Henrietta opened her purse and pulled out a little clasped leather wallet. It looked to Nate like something somebody's grandparent would have. Henrietta pulled out a few bills, counting them. Turning the wallet over, she dumped it out, shaking it.

Nate moved closer, to see over her hands. She glanced up at him. The green in her eyes was a cloudy color, overcast with gray. Her hands, as he looked into them, were like captured birds. Nate felt the wings of little birds in his groin.

"I've got almost five dollars. About enough to buy something to eat tonight and tomorrow. I never should have splurged this afternoon. I don't even have enough money to get on a bus to go home."

Nate had to clear his throat to speak. "Where's home?"

Henrietta squinted her eyes. "I don't want to go there anyway."

"Yeah, but where is it?"

"Goshen, Ohio." There was a sudden sheepishness in her look. "I know. Go ahead. Laugh. Land O' Goshen. My, my, my."

Nate had to hold back his little laugh. "I wasn't even thinking that."

"You were too. I saw you start to laugh."

"No. No. It was just because you acted funny. Like you were ashamed of it or something."

"Well. A lot of people laugh when I tell them. They always say something like, 'Land O' Goshen. Well I swan.'"

"But Ohio isn't down South?"

Henrietta looked at Nate with new interest. "Have you ever been there?"

"No. But I used to live down South. And I know where Ohio is."

"Where did you live?"

"Tennessee. Memphis. I used to live with my grandmother. On her farm."

"You did? I used to live on a farm with my grandmother in Goshen. Outside Cincinnati."

"I guess you wouldn't say we were in Memphis really either. It was Millington, Tennessee. About fifteen or something miles out."

"Same here, but we were out about thirty-five miles. When did you leave Memphis?"

"Oh jeez. I was about thirteen. So I haven't been back there for twelve or thirteen years or something. But I was born in California. In LA. I grew up here mostly, in San Francisco, with my dad. He used to send me to Memphis every summer though, to live with my grandmother. It's strange, because mostly I think of myself as coming from Memphis. I don't know. Maybe I just liked it better, living on the farm."

"Where's your father now?"

She sounded overly solicitous to Nate. He pulled his face back a little. He thought for a moment. "He died." Nate allowed the silence to hang in the air between them. "He died when I was thirteen. Then I went back down to LA, where my mother and brother were, for another two years, and lived with my brother before I decided to get out on my own. I just went around California, working. About six months ago I came back up here, to San Francisco."

"Is your mother still in Los Angeles?"

"She's dead too. A woman stabbed her, in the hospital where she was staying."

"A woman stabbed her in the hospital?" Henrietta sounded incredulous.

"Yeah. She called a woman a nigger and started a fight with her. My mom was crazy. And she hated black people."

"Was your mom from Memphis?"

"No. She was from Brazil. She was part Portuguese and part Indian, she said."

Nate sat for a few quiet moments, as if thinking and not thinking at the same time. "None of them liked black people."

"Who? People from Brazil?"

"No. My father and my mother and my grandmother. My father and my grandmother grew up where it's normal to think like that. But I don't understand about my mother. She was a mixture. I never did know her all that good. But she grew up partly in Brazil, and partly in LA."

"Didn't you stay with her for a while, you said...?"

"Yeah, but when I was little, and then they put her in the state hospital. That's where she stayed. Then I was with my brother down there for a bit."

"Oh." Henrietta would almost have been more content to just sit quiet. Her mind was swimming.

Nate watched her face. It clouded, probably from the things he was telling her. He wanted to move past it. "I guess some people just feel that way about other people. They just don't like them. In a way I can understand it."

Henrietta was jolted. "You mean you believe in it?" She was shocked.

Nate shook his head, then looked her straight in the eyes. "No. I didn't say that. I can't just walk away from everybody in my family. I think they use these ideas to keep fears away. Just the same way they believe that boys should only sleep with girls."

"That's different. That's a biological fact." Henrietta's voice was getting an edge to it.

"If you believe that, then you must have a lot of trouble with San Francisco, with all the different shit that goes on here." Nate almost started to laugh. "They screw any way they can think up." He suddenly embarrassed himself again. He went on, almost to cover up. "They make it part of their politics."

"Well. You know what I mean. I don't think it's right to dislike people because of their skin. Still, I grew up in the middle of it. It's hard to change 'em."

"Well. I just don't believe in it. I think it's evil."

Nate thought he heard a note of self-righteousness in her voice. "Well, that's great. But I've never known anybody in my whole life that didn't have some kind of prejudice. That's all. I just let people be the way they are, or I woulda had nobody." Nate wasn't making a very good impression on her, but suddenly he didn't goddam care. He turned from her and faced out the window, somehow not seeing anything out there at all.

The sun must have suddenly dropped while they weren't paying any attention. "Do you know what time it is?" He reluctantly turned back to her as he asked. Shit! Now she was going to think he was getting tired of waiting.

Nate watched her closely for signs of discontent with him.

Henrietta dug into her purse and brought out an old gold pocket watch. She opened it.

Nate leaned curiously, admiring it.

"Six fifteen." She lifted the watch slightly for him to see better. My grandmother gave it to me." She hesitated heavily. "It was my grandfather's."

She seemed not to want to let him see her face. She closed the watch too quickly.

"You can go now. But I have to wait."

"I didn't want to leave. I was just curious. It's getting dark outside, and I just wasn't thinking about the time. I thought it was earlier was all. I like sitting here talking. You don't mind if I stay?"

"Oh I'm sure you're enjoying talking. After that last conversation. It's alright. You don't have to wait with me."

"But I want to. I was enjoying it."

"I don't see how?"

"Well, if you want me to stop enjoying it, maybe I will, but right now I want to stay... Unless I'm starting to bother you?"

"No. But we can't talk about that topic right now."

They both sat quietly for a few moments. Nate became uncomfortably aware of his appearance. He wished he could cross his legs and hide his boots. He wanted to sit straighter.

"Do you really think the police won't come?" Henrietta cocked her head toward the open part of the lobby. "He said they never come here."

"I don't know. About three months ago there was a guy that got stabbed upstairs. They came quick then. Being the weekend though, maybe they're real busy and this is the kind of thing they put down low on the list. I don't know."

"If they don't help me I'll get kicked out of here. Then I'll have to start sleeping at the Salvation Army or something. If I can even get in there."

Nate pulled himself up. He hadn't been conscious of how scary her situation was. "Now wait a minute. You won't have to sleep out on the street. I can guarantee that. But I wouldn't put it past Benny to call the cops and tell them it was a prank or something. I think it would be better if we went down to the police ourselves."

Henrietta suddenly realized all of the possible combinations of mean things people could be pulling on her. Even Nathan. A deep chill ran through her. Unlike the fear she had felt at the beach, this one had a focus in reality.

Nate saw her shudder. "Hey. I didn't say that's what he did. I just think we ought to go over to the station and report it ourselves. That way you know they're doing something about it. You don't have to just sit here worrying about it."

"But won't they want to see where it happened and everything?"

She seemed suddenly willing to lean more and more on Nate's advice.

"I guess so. But they need to get the report first. Right? And the quickest way it looks like to me is to go over there ourselves. That's foolproof. Right?" Nate wanted desperately to lift Henrietta's cloud a little.

She was too busy trying to keep track of the pieces of her complicated puzzle to notice the nuances of his thoughts.

"After that we can go get something to eat. Okay?"

"I can't do that. I don't have any money."

"Don't worry about it. I do."

"No!" Henrietta was emphatic. "I can't do that."

Nate looked at her blankly for a moment. "Okay." His voice squeezed out weakly. His stomach muscles twitched. Pressure grew behind his eyes. As far as she was concerned, this was the end of her future, right here. He became angry, quickly, inexplicably; both with her, and with her situation. His voice surprised him. "Yeah! And if someday you see me on the street and I need help and you try to help me, I'll just tell you to go away because I can do everything for myself. How's that with you?" The pressure behind his eyes was almost too much. In his mind he was already up from the couch. His body just didn't follow. His muscles may have moved minutely though. He turned away from her. Fuck her. She didn't need him. He sure didn't need her. Nate turned back toward the window. It was truly almost dark now. The two Spanish girls were out in front of the hotel again. They looked like they were working the street. Maybe they weren't. Nate really didn't want to think about it. He heard the couch creak. The cushion under him rocked and the plastic squeaked, like when somebody moves on it.

"Okay."

Nate sat quietly. He thought he wasn't breathing. The couch squeaked again. He turned his head slowly. There was no sign of struggle on her face. There was no sign of tears in her eyes. His almost had them trying to leak out. Her lips were full and firm, pale pink. His slightly blurred eyes noticed that her hair line was perspiring a little bit, shiny. It hid at the base of those heavy strands of red hair.

"But you can't try to tell me what to eat too."

He didn't have in his mind to force her to do anything. "I wasn't planning on it." He paused, half a breath in his lungs. He laughed in his throat.

"What?" Her voice was a questioning laugh.

Nate sat, still thinking about it.

"What?" she asked again.

"Oh." Nate snapped back to awareness. "I was just going to ask—who picks where we go?"

"Well, don't we have to agree on that together?"

"I guess. If we can." The pressure behind his eyes was subsiding, but there was still rolling movement in his stomach.

Henrietta looked across Nate, outside. "I think I'd better go up and get a jacket though. It must be cool out there by now. You did want to go now, didn't you? Is that what you meant?"

"Sure. I thought we'd go get the police thing over with, and then see about eating."

"I've got to go up to my room real quick, then."

Nate moved to the edge of the cushion, his butt barely on it. "I'll go up with you. I need to get my jacket too. Okey-doke?"

As if they had been waiting for cues in an awkward comedy, both of them pushed up from the couch together.

Heading across the sunken lobby, Henrietta controlled her pace so that Nate was always beside her. Neither talked. As they stepped up out of the sunken lobby, Benny pretended to be engrossed in his TV, not noticing them.

In the elevator, Nate wanted to talk, but Henrietta seemed content not to. He reluctantly turned his attention to the graffiti scratched in the elevator-brown paint. He'd read all of it hundreds of times before, out of elevator boredom. He even knew what the scratched-out message by the buttons had said:

MARY GIVES GOOD HEAD

ROOM 214

FREE ANYTIME

Nate speculated. Maybe there wasn't any Mary at all. Or, maybe Mary had scratched it out. Maybe Mary was some dude, and if you knocked on his door, he'd knock you out. Maybe he was Mary and he wouldn't. Nate almost laughed. The elevator stopped at their floor. He held the door while Henrietta got off.

She paced herself to him again in the hallway. "I want to clean up a little bit too. Do you mind waiting?"

Nate almost smiled to himself, but thought better of it. "No. That's okay with me. I'll just wait in my room."

"Are you sure?"

"Sure. Maybe I ought to clean up a little bit too?"

"No. You look fine. I just want to wash some of this beach dirt off. It won't take long, I promise. Wear what you've got on. I think you look fine."

Nate shrugged. He wanted to change. Just into clothes he hadn't been wearing all day. Now it seemed like he couldn't, without appearing stupid. "I'll wait in my room. Knock on the door when you're ready."

"I'm sorry. Are you sure you don't mind?"

"Take your time. No problem. I can read or something."

"Well, I wasn't planning on being that long."

"Whatever. Don't worry about it. It's okay. Just go ahead and do what you need to do." Nate stopped at 306. He tried the knob. For a moment he had the sinking feeling that maybe he'd been robbed too.

"What's the matter?"

"Nothing. For a second I thought my room was unlocked. But it's not."

Henrietta let out a big sigh. "Good!" She stood in the hall.

Nate unlocked his door, but only barely pushed it open.

Henrietta couldn't see in.

"Go do your thing and I'll be waiting when you get through."

"Okay." Henrietta stood for a moment, curious. Nate didn't move. He was obviously waiting for her to leave. "I'll see you in a few minutes then."

"Okay."

She turned down the hall. At her room, Henrietta glanced back toward Nate's. He was leaning out of the doorway, watching her. She smiled. "I'll hurry up."

"You don't have to."

"I will!"

"Okay."

She pushed into her room and closed the door.

twenty

Nate's door slammed harder than he meant it to. He stood inside for a bit, quiet. He didn't know what he was thinking. There was a pleasant buzz in his chest. He moved over and sat on the bed. He stared at the photograph of the house he had worked on down in Carmel. Momentarily, It was almost like he was standing back out on the end of the rocks, watching the sea undulate around him, all blue, crashing just below him.

Loud yelling splashed up from the street. Nate wrinkled his brow, got up, and went over to poke his head out the window. The rapid movements of two men in the gas station caught his eye. They seemed to be arguing over who would get to use one of the pumps first. One had the nozzle in his hands. He was small. He looked like the kind of family man who might work as a quiet machinist in a factory. The one making all the noise was fifty or sixty pounds heavier, round and menacing. His head bobbed under an orange ball cap as he yelled. He looked dangerous to Nate. Everybody else in the station stood still, pumping their gas, watching. One of the attendants was standing in the door of the store there, anxious, not wanting to have anything to do with a fight, not knowing what to do.

The big guy suddenly grabbed in the middle of the hose and held it so the machinist couldn't quite reach the nozzle to his tank. Then the big one flipped the pump handle off with his thick, meaty hand. Nate stopped breathing. After a moment, the big guy threw the taut hose to the pavement. The little man had to grab it with both hands as it sprung on its cable. Quiet now, the big man swung around and yanked open the door of his tall pickup and began reaching around inside. Nate's back tightened.

Only a week before, just below his room, two men got in a fight over a parking space. One pulled out a pistol and put a bullet in the other one's leg. Two kinds of screaming had filled the air after the explosion; the screaming of the guy who got hit, and the screaming of the shooter's tires peeling down the street. Nate pulled his head back in and yanked down the sash. He pulled the shade and stood silently, trying to forget the chaos in the street out there. A chaos that could suck anybody into its vortex. He turned from the window and was almost against his dresser. The toes of his boots pushed against the FINE WOODWORKING magazines stacked under the chest. His eyes couldn't focus on the blue NASA photograph of Monterey Bay he had hung behind the dresser.

A loud, hard sound, almost like a crack hit his ears and he jumped. Then he slumped. His veins became jelly. Pain shot through him, as if the bullet had torn its way through his chest. He couldn't turn in the direction of the window.

There was a second loud crack. It had been coming from a different direction. Nate was confused. He glanced nervously around the room. A third crack rocked his room door. He jumped across to it and pulled quickly. Henrietta stood expectant in the hall. Nate's arms shook. He kept his hand on the door jamb, unable to speak. Her face was fresh. Her eyes seemed different, darker. He looked to find the freckle on her lip. She had covered it with a burnt red lipstick. She was wearing a turquoise blouse that clung like a film, and black slacks. She had a white sweater on her arm.

"I'm ready."

Nate didn't say anything immediately.

"Is something wrong?"

"No. I guess I wasn't...." He turned his head toward the window and kept his hand on the door jamb.

She fumbled with her sweater and purse. "Do you still want to go? Or did you change your mind?"

Nate had to turn his attention back. His eyes dropped to her full breasts, and then down to her black slacks. "I guess I wasn't expecting you so quick."

"Is something wrong with these clothes?"

"No. You look really nice. I just haven't changed yet myself."

"You look fine to me. I told you you could just wear what you had on."

"No." Nate glanced back down at her fresh clothes. "I don't want to do that. Time just went faster than I thought it would."

Henrietta peeked under his dropping face. "Something is wrong isn't it?"

"No. I guess the fight across the street made me nervous. I thought when you knocked on the door it was a gun going off."

"What fight?"

"Oh. Some guys over in the gas station were fighting about a gas hose. I saw one of them go into his truck and I was sure he was getting a gun. I thought I heard the gun going off. I guess I just didn't want to look out there and see somebody laying on the ground with a hole in their chest or something."

Henrietta tried to push into the room. "If somebody got shot...."

Nate held the door tight. "No. Nobody got shot. I thought when you knocked on the door that it was a gun going off. I just thought...people are crazy around here."

Henrietta could see into Nate's room now. It was not appreciably different from hers. The layout and the furniture were the same. On the wall by the window was a large photograph of a house perched on a rock by the ocean. She wondered why he had that. Stacks of magazines were pushed under the dresser. She was curious about them. She could see part of the bed with a striped Mexican blanket on it. She could, of course, see the closed window behind the bed, with its shade pulled down. The closet door stood slightly open. A white towel hung on the closet rack.

"Do you want me to go wait in my room for a few minutes? While you get ready? I don't mind."

"Nah. I guess I'm ready now." Nate pushed the door. "Let me get my jacket."

Henrietta had to back into the hall to let Nate get into his closet. Out in the hall, she felt strangely alone, listening to his rustling behind the door. Who was this strange man? She almost wanted to lean her ear and listen. She fought the urge.

When Nathan came back out the room was dim. He quickly pulled the door behind him. She kept sneaking glances toward him. Lately, everyone seemed strange to her. Maybe it was just her thinking that was strange, but it was obvious to her that she couldn't totally trust anybody right now.

In the elevator, on the way down, neither of them talked. When the gated car hit bottom, they glanced at each other, but Nate quickly looked away.

Someone had the lobby TV on. It was screaming "believe it or not...." Nate suddenly wanted to go back up to his room. His neck and hairline were prickly with sweat. The chances for humiliation were too many. He would have done better just to offer her some money. He saw Benny throw an angry face as they passed by the office. Henrietta didn't look up.

Henrietta began to wonder if Nathan was all there. She had made a strict pact with herself when she moved into the hotel to stay away from all the men in there. Was her situation making her reckless? Maybe she was becoming self-destructive. As he held the front door, Henrietta snuck a quick look at Nathan. She tried to memorize his face in the light that poured from the lobby. He was a good-looking man. Something about his face was strong, even under his boyish freckles. She felt drawn to his spots the way she felt drawn to horses and dogs with spots. They seemed somehow like children that would never grow up. Nathan's nose was perfect, but his chin was just the slightest bit weak. Not really weak, but not protruding the way they always thought it should in movies. She followed his lead as he turned right out of the hotel. His hair had become dark in the night, but she knew it was kind of a lighter brown-red. She remembered it being almost like a cocker spaniel's hair, ruddy butterscotch. Before they passed out of the light, she peeked again, and it was not that pale at all.

Nate turned to Henrietta. She was looking at him. "What?" He laughed self-consciously.

"Nothing." She said.

"What's wrong? Is my hair screwed up? Shit! I forgot to comb it."

"There's nothing wrong with your hair. I was just looking at it. Trying to decide what the color was. That's all."

Nate felt the skin prickle at his hair line again. He couldn't look back at her. They walked quietly out South Van Ness, toward Seventeenth.

Henrietta felt a little trepidation going in that direction. It was unfamiliar, darker.

Suddenly, Nate spoke. "Your name is Henrietta, right?"

Henrietta felt a little chilling ripple. "I didn't tell you that."

"I thought I heard you say it on the phone. Telling the police your name."

See, there it was again. The immediate suspicion and the instant distrust. Henrietta checked if she was overreacting. "Oh..." she said and looked up the street. What few businesses were up this way were closed. It was a little lonely. Without warning, Nate moved quickly across the sidewalk, in toward Henrietta, almost as if he was trying to pin her against the wall of the building. Henrietta's heart started pumping rapidly in her chest. She stopped, ready to react.

Completely unaware of her fears, Nate absently stuck out his arm to lead her around the corner of the building.

Henrietta stopped in her tracks, and then quickly realized what he was doing, and was suddenly ashamed of herself. She saw, briefly, that if she wasn't careful, Nate might quickly gain an innocent power over her, without even trying. She took a few rapid steps to catch back up with him.

A strong breeze blew down Seventeenth Street into their faces. It ruffled Nate's hair. It washed his face with cool. He thought of salt air. Her butt spread across the seat and the khaki fabric of her short pants wrinkled and unwrinkled perfectly as she pedaled the bicycle away from him. He wanted to grab out, protectively, as if a line were attached to the back of the bicycle, like an old dentist joke where they tie a string to your tooth and to the bumper of a car. This line was attached to Nate's tongue. It yanked at him as she pedaled away. His tongue popped out of his mouth. Amazing. Behind it followed the rosary of his internal organs; his heart wrenched out first, and then his lungs, his stomach and his intestines. He became an empty, shapeless bag, about to fall to the ground, trying to wave her down, completely without the ability to move or to speak. The cool ocean breeze across the sandy beach carried the sounds of seals barking in the distance, and the ammonia odor of rotting seaweed.

"Nate? Is something wrong?"

Nate turned toward Henrietta, half-startled. "No. Why?"

"I don't know. All of a sudden I felt like you were somewhere else. You don't want to do this with me do you?"

"Yes I do. I really like being out in this weather."

"Then maybe you just don't want to be with me. You know you don't have to take me to dinner just because you feel sorry for me."

"I know that." The breeze pulled Henrietta's hair back from her face, revealing her neck. It seemed tiny to Nate, vulnerable.

"I don't want you to have to pay my way, like we're on a date or something."

Nate suddenly changed the subject. "Why don't we just go to the police station and take care of your business. Then we can worry about that."

Henrietta watched his face again. Light from a lone car coming up behind them silhouetted their moving forms, projecting them as giants on the wall to the right of them. "Do you really think the police will care about my money, Nate?"

Nate was taken aback, hearing his name like that again. He liked it. It gave his name an importance it hadn't seemed to have before. "I don't know."

"Do you think they'll even try to do anything?"

"I don't know, Henrietta. You have to report it though, don't you? You can't let it go like nothing happened."

"I'm starting to believe what that creep was saying."

"Benny? Shit. He's just...."

"I know. He has other ideas on his mind. He wants me to fail. He wants me to be out of money."

"Don't think about him."

Henrietta had fallen into perfect step with Nate. They moved in unison as they crossed Mission Street. There were a few women lined up on the walls still, and their pimp was in the doorway of the corner store, all of them on the lookout for tricks. Nate did his best to ignore their existence.

Henrietta went on, "I know all about him. He's tried to talk me into things before, to get my rent lowered. I just couldn't stand the thought. But I do have to say that in the lobby tonight I was trying to imagine what it would be like."

"Jesus!" Nate stopped on the sidewalk, just at the curb. He waited for the light to change so they could cross Seventeenth.

"Well. Sometimes you do what you have to."

"Yeah. But...." Nate tried to shove the picture of Benny and Henrietta from his mind. The thought was like a determined cat he was trying to throw out of the house, and it clung to his consciousness, claws in, nearly driving him to distraction with sharp pricks in the surface of his mind. Nate shook himself to get rid of it.

"Anyway. I have to admit I thought about it for a moment. But that's all. He's nothing but a pig."

It put Nate off his equilibrium to think of her being so expeditious, so realistic.

Henrietta wanted to keep talking. She felt comfortable with him. He did act a little strange from minute to minute though. She watched him as they crossed Seventeenth in silence.

twenty-one

Martin pushed up on his paw and swung his head, shaking his hair around him in the small cave. He loved its light sting on his back and chest; bringing life to his skin. The fog and cold night air had invaded his sleep. He pushed himself up, grabbing the cane. He stepped into the opening, snatching the boots up in his other paw. He leaned out in the quiet dark. The night air brushed his free skin, rolling down the alley past him. He could see dim clouds above the alley, in the slice of sky, and dark over the peaks. With his right hand he swung his cane in an arc and let it fly. It thumped the side of a building and clacked several times on the pavement. He swung his boots too and let them bounce off the building directly across from him. He shook his whole body.

Martin stepped down from the ledge. The stony path tried to cut the thick skin of his foot pads. His toe claws clicked on the hard surface. He felt them try to dig in. Settling into his challenge stance he could feel the coiled power in his legs. A breeze riffled the hair on his body again. He felt the electric current of life in his blood. The heavy skin of his face was tight in the cool air. He lumbered down the tiny canyon. He had nothing to fear.

His movement was perfect in its strength and the sure knowledge of his power. Martin emerged from the small canyon into a larger one. It was brighter, as if the moon breathed light down into it. There were others moving in this canyon, but he feared no one now.

twenty-two

Just the other side of Seventeenth, Nate and Henrietta passed a teenage couple, leaning against the metal gate over the front of the car repair shop. They were kissing in youthful oblivion, every kiss like it was their last. Henrietta's arm brushed Nate's. He turned to her. She smiled. He smiled to himself.

A woman screamed close by. Nate's eyes went up, fearful. His blood shot through him like ice-water. Just in front of them, in the opening of Clarion Alley, a naked man was stumbling in the light. He held his arms crazily out in front of him. His hair was long and black. A woman on the other side of the small alley backed out into the street. She had her hands up, half-covering her dark face.

Henrietta started to laugh. She moved closer. The man was brown. His nose had a hawkish native masculinity. The skin of his face looked solid, stiffly set in its expression.

A charge in the air grabbed Nate, like one of those electrical accidents that won't let go until it throws you to the ground. Henrietta suddenly stepped forward. He reached to pull her back, but she was already out of his range. He had to jump up next to her. A small Hispanic family stood on the other side of the alley, pointing and laughing at the man. The beginning of a crowd was starting to clot and gather behind them. They could have just as well been at a circus. Nate felt again the pinch of that electrical power. He wanted to put Henrietta behind him for protection, and he wanted to hold her, for a ground.

On the other side of the alley, people were pointing at the naked Indian, laughing. It reminded Henrietta of the old-time bear baiting's she had seen in books. She swallowed a slip of fear. Her eye caught a teenager on the edge of the just-formed crowd. He had a beer bottle in his hand. Something in his face made her nervous; one of those feisty street-fighters. She moved closer.

Henrietta moved closer to the danger. Nate reached to stop her. Something fell and broke. Glass on the pavement. He stretched and touched Henrietta's arm. He gripped her forearm gently, but ready to be firmer. His eyes searched the crowd on the other side of the alley. He could hear a small group starting to grow on the sidewalk behind he and Henrietta. His eyes were quick enough to see a young Cholo throw another bottle. It bounced off the Indian's naked chest with a low thump and dropped to the ground with a crash.

Henrietta saw splintered glass crowd around the Indian's bare feet. She shuddered. One piece landed over near her shoe. It was dark, dark brown, almost like his skin. It could have been a piece of him that had been chipped from his rock body. He squatted and grabbed the broken neck. He held it tight. He almost reared up, as if to threaten the crowd. He let out an attempt at a roaring noise. Henrietta wanted to wrap him in something. She wanted to get him out of there.

Several people screamed. Henrietta moved first. She jumped toward the Indian and yelled. "Somebody's got to stop him!" Nate grabbed to hold her back. She whipped to him and yelled. "Somebody's got to stop him!"

Nate felt like he had been torn open. He leapt forward, using her as leverage. Then the asshole stabbed himself in the chest with a stump of the beer bottle. Blood spurted in small gushes out onto his dark skin and ran down to the asphalt. Nate's skin rippled, from his ass up over his head. He had to keep Henrietta from getting in there. He tried to push himself off but now she held to him, wanting to go with him. Nate saw the shriveled right leg. He recognized the Indian from the BART station. His heart expanded, as if ready to burst out of his chest.

"Stop him!" Henrietta screamed again. Her hands flew free, Nate leapt across the asphalt and blindly grabbed out, getting an arm in his hand. His skin jumped when he thought of being slashed himself. "You've got the wrong arm, Nate!" He heard Henrietta holler. The slippery Indian swung the hand with the bottle again. This time he was thrown off-balance by Nate. The slashing edge of the bottle hit awkwardly on the Indian's neck. Blood immediately spurted in a stream out into the air.

The blood washed over Nate. His foot slipped and the two of them almost fell. Nate managed to get a hold on the other arm. It was slippery with thick, almost gelatinous, blood. The muscles were loosening as he gripped at the arm. Nate tried to keep the Indian from falling. His face contorted and his heavily expelling breath hit Nate's cheek. Nate grabbed wherever he could hold. It was all slippery. Henrietta was next to him now. She grabbed the other arm. The Indian fell anyway, and pulled Nate down with him. "Nate, Nate!" Henrietta cried, almost in his ear. "Be careful!" Then there was a quiet moment, and it seemed the crowd around them let out a universal whoosh of noise. No noise was coming from the bloody naked body. Henrietta pulled Nate up to his feet. The Indian was leaking blood slower and slower now. She wanted to think of something to use for bandages. But that was useless now. There was no way to save him with his neck cut like that. She looked at Nate. He only stared at the open gash. He looked pale. They both looked around them. Everyone had gone quiet, and their faces all held the same expression. The kid who threw the bottle was gone.

"Nate?"

Nate kept his eyes on the open flesh. Henrietta pulled her sweater from the ground where it had fallen. She quickly put it over the Indian's chest and neck. It covered the lower part of his face. The white seemed to glow on him there in the streetlight.

"Nate?" She reached out with her bloody hand and took him by the chin. "Nate?" She pulled his face around toward her. His eyes passed through her like she was a looking glass into another world. She squeezed his face with her hand. Blood was drying on her fingers, cracking her skin as she moved. Nate had blood drying on his face.

Nate heard a voice slide past his head, as if it were the surface of water he was going under. His body glided toward the bottom of a deep narrow pool. His feet would land in softness.

"Nate! Nate! Nate!"

Houdini in a safe world, he was in a glass tank, curled on a sandy bottom. Somebody banged on the glass, wanting him out. He wanted to stay.

"Nate!" Henrietta shook him by the arm. What the hell was happening to him? She looked around her, for help from someone.

"Oh no!" Someone screamed from over Henrietta's shoulder. She spun her head back to see. A woman held her hands to her face, her voice modulated by terror and pain. "Oh no...Oh no...."

"Somebody help me! Quick!" Henrietta said as she looked around at the staring faces "I need somebody to help me!" No one else moved. Their mouths hung open, all 'O's.

"Did somebody call an ambulance? I need help here!" She said.

An ambulance wouldn't help now. What was she thinking? They needed the police. Henrietta still held Nate's arm. She felt him vibrate. It wasn't much, but he moved. She turned back to him. His eyes were still glassy. "Nate? Don't leave me now. I need your help. Please?"

He was in some kind of shock. She helped him the short distance to the other sidewalk. She thought she saw the boy who had thrown the bottle down the block, heading toward Eighteenth with a couple of other guys, his team jacket a little too dark to read. People at the edge of the alley crowded back reluctantly, like shuffling cows in a stockyard. There was room for Nate to sit, just out of the spill of blood. Henrietta helped him down, then looked up to find a phone. She couldn't trust that any of these crowding, open-mouthed people would call the police. She saw the sign for a little market just beyond the crowd on the sidewalk, and started to push that way. As soon as people saw she was covered with blood, they gave her the same shocked wide berth they would have given a leper. For a moment, she was almost glad she was covered with blood.

Nate tried to fight up from the sidewalk, mumbling, "I've got to get up." Halfway to his feet, he glanced at the Indian, lying in the greasy pool of blood. Sickness forced its way up through his throat, coming out of him.

He turned his head instinctively and heaved out to the side. It almost threw him back to the ground.

Henrietta heard Nate heaving and glanced back quickly. Throwing up wasn't all that terrible. Henrietta pushed through the crowd and saw a telephone at the bright doors of the Mission Market. A great big guy in a t-shirt and leather vest, big tattoos all over his arms, was on the phone, waving his free hand around to emphasize a point to whoever he was talking to. Voices all around Henrietta were discussing the accident, as she tried to get through the group.

"I think that red-haired guy attacked the other one with a broken bottle. They were fighting when I got here."

Henrietta yelped quickly at the voice behind her, still moving forward. "He was trying to help! Stupid idiot!"

"Jesus. What a fucking mess." Another voice said. "Let's get out of here."

"Why is that one naked? Did somebody call the cops? An ambulance?"

"I'm going to." Henrietta called out, as if the disembodied voice who had asked the question would understand her disembodied answer. By the time Henrietta was through the shuffling lookers, the phone was free, and the big guy was out near the curb, smoking a cigarette and looking up and down the street like he was waiting for something. She headed straight for the phone. At that moment, two short young Hispanic guys came out of the market, tightly wrapped paper bags in their hands, oversized work shirts hanging down almost to their knees. One was twisting his paper bag tighter and tighter, while the other stopped at the phone and started to pull it out of the cradle. "Don't use that phone!" Henrie called out as she hurried up. They both turned to her, and looked her up and down strangely.

"Lady, what the fuck happened to you?" He asked as he stepped back from the phone, and she could see a beeper in his hand with his paper-wrapped beer. "I have to call 911. Someone's hurt over there." She pointed, and the guy looked in the direction she was pointing, just for a moment, then back at all the blood on her.

"You're covered with blood. Are you okay?" A disembodied voice came from over near the street. Henrietta looked that way, and the big guy was staring at her, at her chest. She shook her head that she was fine. "Yeah, I'm fine," then she looked down at herself again, and was shocked again to see the thickening blood.

"Good. I already called the cops. They're coming." He was smiling at her. Henrie just stared back at him. His voice was like a boy permanently stuck halfway through puberty. She couldn't tell if what he was saying was true, a joke, a little hoax, or what. She turned back to the phone, and the guy with the beeper was now dialing it, turned from her. She looked back at the big guy. "I called them. I did." He said, earnestly. Then he held out his big meaty hand. There were tattoos on his knuckles. Letters. V and E were all she saw. "My name's Billy." He said, in that unfinished voice.

Henrietta didn't know what to do. The sounds of sirens started off in the night, not far away.

Nate tried to get up from the sidewalk again. He forced his muscles to respond and he stood. His head was filled with a deadly gas. He had to fight out of the dizziness. Somebody grabbed him by the arm and held him strongly.

"You're not going anywhere pal. "

"What the hell?" He yanked at his arm, still half-blind. Nate was almost spun off-balance by the strong grip on his upper arm. The man beside him had a round flat face. He was short and stocky, with the look of a brick-layer. His grasp was dead-strong.

"Just stay right here. You're not going anywhere." The bricklayer said.

"Jesus!" Nate didn't feel like fighting with the guy. While the bricklayer gripped his arm, Nate tried to look for Henrietta. He passed his eyes over the alley opening, not letting them rest on anything. He pushed up onto his toes and tried to see into the crowd behind him. Henrietta's red head was bobbing in the light spilling out of the Mission Market. She looked like she was talking to a big tattooed guy. What the hell was she doing? "Henrietta!" There must have been too much noise. Her head did not turn his way. "Henrietta!" He had trouble staying on his toes. The round guy held his arm in a rock grip. Her head turned his way, just before he was pulled back down to his flat feet.

Nate was about to get mad. The little, rock-hard son of a bitch was getting to him. "Get the fuck off my fucking arm, Goddammit!"

"Settle down pal. You're going to stay right here until the police come. So, you may as well relax."

Henrietta was caught, not knowing whether to take the guy's hand or not. She heard Nate yell her name. It sounded so plaintive, like a lost calf.

Billy seemed disappointed as Henrietta spun back around. Henrietta heard squawking over a loudspeaker. A fast-approaching siren cut into Henrietta's flesh. Then there was a flurry of sirens coming from all directions. She suddenly stopped. Everything was catching up with her, everything was moving quickly around her.

Did Nate need her? People were packed between her and him. Henrietta stood in the middle of the crowd, suddenly alone now. Her chest felt wet. She looked down again in the confused light from the street and café. The blood soaking her blouse and slacks had turned a throbbing, thickening black in a weird pulsing light. She felt sad, sorry, violated; she felt she herself was violating. The heavy engine of the ambulance and its rasping beep penetrated through all other sounds and thoughts. Henrietta looked up to see the big orange and white truck backing into the alley entrance. It dwarfed the crowded people and overwhelmed the claustrophobic little scene.

Someone yelled for people to stand back.

She began to push back through the crowd, toward the alley. Over heads, Henrietta could see the medics were getting back into their truck, with gruesome looks on their faces.

She made it to the edge of the tiny clearing at the scene of the tragedy. There were maybe seven policemen, some were trying to push the fascinated clump of lookers back, and others were gathered around the body under the sheet or talking to people, gathering information with their little notepads. The Indian was covered now with a blood-soaked sheet. It was over for him. Now everybody else was just swarming around him like flies.

Henrietta couldn't think about that, or it would make her scream. Where was Nate? She scanned the crowd as the ambulance labored out of the alley, grinding its engine and blipping its siren to clear a path. She stood just back from the edge of the blood-soaked pavement, peering around. When the ambulance was gone, Henrietta saw Nate out in the street, leaning against the back of a police car, a policeman so close she was sure Nate felt threatened. His head was down, as if he was guilty of something. Another policeman at the front of the patrol care listened closely to a short, fat man. The fat man was pointing at Nate, almost like he was accusing him of something. Henrietta called Nathan's name. He didn't look up. She hurried out to him.

When she was near, Henrietta called Nate's name again. The policeman with Nate turned, jumpy. Henrietta stopped, her hand halfway out, the breath suddenly dry in her body.

The officer's face immediately fell when he saw her. "Aw shit! Not another one!" He swung quickly toward where the ambulance was pulling down the street. "Medic! Hal, stop that ambulance!"

Henrietta wanted to reach out but held herself back. "No. I'm okay. I'm not hurt."

He quickly looked her over. The van was too far anyhow.

"I came over to tell you what happened to my friend and me."

The policeman pointed with his heavy thumb. "Is this your friend here?"

"Yes. His name is Nate."

"Okay. Stand right there and don't talk. We'll get your statement in a minute. As soon as that man is finished."

The fat man continued his story. "So, this guy was sitting on the curb all bloody, throwing up. I figured he musta had something to do with it, so when he started to get up and I thought he was going to leave I grabbed his arm and made sure he stayed put."

"Then you didn't see him involved in a fight with the dead man?"

"No. But you can tell by looking at him. I just put two and two together."

Henrietta couldn't keep quiet. She couldn't wait. "He was trying to stop him from stabbing himself. That's how he got all bloody. Nathan was trying to get the piece of bottle out of his hand. He just wasn't fast enough."

Nate was oddly quiet during this exchange. Henrietta wondered why he didn't defend himself. It was like he wanted others to decide his fate for him.

At the edge of the crowd, maybe ten feet away, Henrietta saw a young Hispanic girl, a teenager, pulling her arm out of the grasp of an older boy. She said something to him, and made a calming hand gesture, palm down, as she came toward the policeman with Nate.

"Sir...." At first, because her voice was so quiet, the policeman paid no attention to the young girl who had come up to them.

Nate heard her, though. He looked up at the sound of the quiet voice, and noticed her. She was beautiful. He could see that, even in this strange, unstill light. She had a fleshy but fine-boned quiet face. She looked into Nate's eyes for a moment. Hers were dark and inscrutable, warmly innocent. She looked back to the police officer. "Sir?"

This time, the policemen turned to the girl. She spoke again. "I saw what happened. From the beginning." This quiet confident voice somehow demanded their attention.

"You did?" The cop asked her.

The girl looked at Nate, then Henrietta for a moment, then back to the police officer. She nodded.

"Well, can you tell me what you saw?" The policeman asked and looked from her to Nate and back.

Nate strained to hear over all the other noise, including the rushing sound of his own blood in his head. It was all fuzzy to him.

"Yes sir." She paused. "The man," she pointed toward the bloody sheet in the alley, where policemen were inspecting and talking. "He was in the entrance to the alley... Dancing and making noise." She halted for a moment, then started again. "He wasn't wearing any clothes. Some people were laughing at him, and a boy threw a bottle at him...it broke on the street near his feet. He picked up a piece of it and..." Her eyes were cast to the ground now. "He started to stab himself in the chest with it." She briefly again looked up at Nate with her coal-dark eyes. "This man tried to stop him, but it was impossible. He seemed to want to hurt himself. The other one, I mean." She turned her head toward Henrietta. "She tried to help him too. She was with this man." The girl glanced back and forth between Henrietta and Nate, and then to the officer. "They were the only ones who tried to help him."

Nate's eyes were on the girl. He couldn't speak with all the noise, both inside him and outside him.

"Okay. I'm going to ask all of you to go down to the precinct so we can make reports on what happened." He turned to the girl. "Would you do that?"

She nodded her head. "Can I call talk to my brother over there first, so he can tell my mother I'll be late?"

"Of course. You can also call her from the station." He turned away from the young girl. "Okay." He took Nate's arm. "I want you to get in my car. And I want you," he pointed at Henrietta, "to go to that policeman at the front of the car." He pointed at Hal at the front of the car, and gently guided the young girl that way too with a fatherly hand. He called to Hal again. Hey Hal! Can you get a couple of cars to take these folks down to the station?"

"Sure! How many?"

"Get those three in separate cars!"

A third policeman came over to the little group to lead Henrietta, the girl and the fat man away. Henrietta watched Nate's face as she left. Nate looked from her to the girl. He looked awful sorry, awful guilty, awful sad to her. Henrietta's heart went out to Nate. She was also a little angry, and shocked at how weird and confused things could become so quickly.

The policeman opened the back door to let Nate in. He thought he might as well get in. He was finally on his way down, and nothing could stop it anyway. Nate scooted across the flat plastic seat cover, over near the middle, and the cop slammed the door. Things were quiet for a moment. Then the car's radio scraped the air, like a knife on Nate's thin nerves. A woman's voice squawked something so fast and so loud that Nate couldn't understand a word. Nate's policeman was over talking to another cop in a suit. The yellow blinking light on the roof of the car that had been mesmerizing him had now lost its effect. He could sit and watch everything, almost as if he was suspended in a gel full of squawking sounds, watching a busy world play out around the car.

The policeman hurried back to the car and slid in. He started the engine and pulled out. Nate didn't see where Henrietta was; he turned back and saw the young girl as they passed her sitting in the other car, like an angel of honesty and duty.

She had seen all of it with those black velvet eyes. From the second he saw her, Nate focused on her steadiness, and she gave him enough strength to stay upright. His chest pulled tight as their car moved away, speeding down the dark, sparkling street.

twenty-three

The car stopped heavily, nosed in, not even an inch shy of the tall concrete wall. Well, this is where he had started off for anyway. In the car next to them, the fat man stared at Nate. Nate looked quickly away while his cop sat up front; not talking, filling out rustling papers. Nate was afraid to move for fear of the squeaky noise the plastic seat cover would make. He only wanted quiet as the rush in his head subsided. Another car pulled next to them. Her tiny head was dark in the back of it. Then her face reflected light from a bright bulb high above the cars. She became a dusky distant moon. She seemed so vulnerable, even in her determination, in the back seat of that fearful car. Then Henrietta's car pulled in one more over. She appeared much larger, so much brighter over there, through the succession of car windows. Her red hair turned by the lighting to a saffron cloud surrounding her pale face, and the tiny dark girl nearer. And here he was now, shivering in a police car in the San Francisco night.

"Okay. Let's go!" Nate's cop spoke.

Nate had to wait for the policeman to let him out of the back. There were no handles or knobs. He would have laughed if the air hadn't started to go bad in the car.

More bright lights and more noise and more people. Nate was steered, in front of the policeman, through an open steel door, into an almost blin-dingly hard room. He was pushed gently to the nearest end of a long table in the center of the room.

The girl was led to the other end, where a big desk phone sat, stolid. She tried to lower herself quietly to her seat, but the wooden chair squealed and echoed in the big tile-walled room. They were the only ones there so far. Nate stood and watched her. She kept her eyes down. Nate was gently shown to a chair near the doors, facing out. He didn't try to sit down quietly.

Car doors slammed outside. First, the fat guy, and then Henrietta, were led into the room by their drivers. Nate looked into Henrietta's eyes. She seemed to be searching his face for signs he was okay. All he could think to do was suddenly cry. But he couldn't do that. The way she looked, all bloody, her clothes twisted, he could have screamed for her if she couldn't for herself. He didn't know if he had led her into this, or if she had led him into it. Her cop yelled, "They're all yours Manini and Richards!" Henrietta winced a little at the noise. Richards and Manini must have made some kind of quiet side joke as they came out, both trying to stifle laughs. The cop pointed to the woman, "Manini," he said, then pointed at Henrietta. As Manini took Henrietta, Richards took the fat guy. Nate's driver handed Richards his papers and returned to the door and stood for a moment, looking the room over. "Richards, keep an eye on this guy, Nathan." He pointed at Nate before going back out to the cars. After saying something quietly to Manini, Henrietta was taken into a room past Nate, down the table, and past the girl. Nate turned to watch her leave. The fat man was taken to one of two small cubicles, just across from Nate, below the wire-covered windows. Almost everything in the room was hard. The walls were a hard-surfaced, mustardy glazed brick. The floors were flecked linoleum over concrete. Your body jarred when you walked on it. Nate looked back again, and the soft girl sat quietly at the far end of the long hard oak table, answering questions that another policeman asked her in his lowered voice. She was sincere and honest, like an example from a high-school civics lesson.

twenty-four

"Nobody feels any pain

Tonight as I stand inside the rain"

Henrietta had come back into the brick and concrete-hard room through a door down at the far end of the table. Her blouse looked wet, but she still had blood all over her. What had they been doing back there? They weren't searching her, were they? Why wasn't she allowed to clean that blood off? Nate wanted to stand up and yell at them. 'She's innocent! Can't you just take her home?' But his mind was like a Peter Lorre movie. By trying to move them off her he would be putting them on her scent more tightly. And he was the fucking one they wanted anyway. His heart was the one with a mark branded into its dense, throbbing fibers.

Manini led Henrietta And length of the room again, down to the other gray cubicle past Nate. She was still watching for the sign of breaking in his eyes. He knew what she was looking for. His was the chest going soft in fear.

Nate dropped his eyes to the table. He heard the soft voice, "Maria... varez." Maria Alvarez?

Henrietta's feet and part of her black legs were all that Nate could see protruding from her cubicle. Her tan shoes were flat on the floor. She must have been sitting straight and proper. The tan shoes sat in knowledge of him, seeing him more clearly than he saw them. Nate was beginning to know himself for the criminal sinner he was.

His father's son.

And his mother's son.

"Mr. Ring" The cop called his name loudly. Nate shivered, He wanted to jump and run out the door of the station. He could hop in a police car and squeal out of the driveway, backward, and away down the street backward, dangerously fast.

Of course, they would pull out their guns and shoot him for even trying it. The blue people in the room bristled with weapons.

Nate stood up slowly from the chair. "That's me." Swift hand motions from the policeman caused Nate to step lightly toward where the serious man stood, weighted to the floor by all the gadgets he carried on that fat cop belt. The gun, with its hard wood-clad butt riding high out of the thick leather holster, displaying brutish blue-black steel of seriousness, made Nate shiver again.

The girl, Maria, got up, chair scraping the floor, and her cop led her to the front and out of the room, presumably free to go home. Nate wanted to go home, too, with Henrietta.

twenty-five

The door to his room stood open. Nate was hanging out the open window, trying to arrange his dripping clothes on the sill. The street below was quiet, moving in silent waves. He kept wanting to turn and watch for Henrietta to pass, but he didn't.

A sudden, silent, wave grabbed him from the ragged edge of his high rock, washing him down into the sea with it.

Algin seaweed, as smooth as the sweet skin of a child of the moon was wrapping itself around him. The soft inexorable strength of the moon pulled heavy waves over him.

Mona. Mona. Mona. If the sound within him could come out and be heard, then all the tangled bodies all over the world would stop and listen, longing too.

He wanted to leap back onto shore and dig into the land and find a place to grow and not be pulled out again.

"Nate! What are you doing?"

He hadn't heard her come in. Nate struggled back in the window, almost losing his wet jacket which was dragging against the rough brick of the building. Henrietta's eyes cast heavily on him. Nate could see her checking him out, concerned. She was making certain of every move of his skin.

The groan still hung in his chest. It was trying to find a shape in the form of Henrietta's name, but it couldn't gel itself in his voice. His silence made fear expand in her green eyes. He was also aware of the wet denim jacket tugging heavily at his fingers. Cool moisture evaporated in his hand. He let the jacket go. There was nothing else to do. He had to move. Even a sturdy, patient beach can be washed away by a rough sea. The shell of Nate's torso was not human. He could almost feel his extremities, his hands and feet, those freezing claws. His eyes were awash in seawater.

He tried to twist the tight, unformed moan into her name. He could feel himself reach and hold her moist warmth. She had been in the sun all day, she smelled fresh across the space. He could see the strain for motion under her steady skin. Henrietta. He had wanted her name to be a statement, to sound solid, to sound confident. He hadn't really meant it to come out as a moan! That was no gift. He was pulled, softly, insistently in and out... In and out... In and out... Henrietta....

"Henrietta...."

The policeman's presence had been oppressive in Nate's cubicle, the largeness of that dark blue uniform. Nate, with his head down, almost leaned his shoulder against the cop's heavy, laden middle, to push him away.

■　■　■

His stiff cold body stumbled forward. He could sense her warmth and moisture coming through the chenille robe, through his own robe. He could feel the moisture evaporating from the tendrils of her just-washed hair. She raised her arms and Nate moved against her. He could measure her shape with the front of his body, where her breasts pushed out under the nubby blue fabric, where her belly rounded a little and she went back in at the top of her legs. He sensed hesitation in her, but they were now locked in the embrace. She squeezed him until the stone in his chest wanted to pop out.

twenty-six

Something in Henrietta had changed in the last twenty-four hours. Lowering herself slowly to her bed, she opened the stiff, blue paper. She could smell that cool Shalimar coming up from the paper, from so close, like Grandma was holding her tight and her chin was on Grandma's shoulder.

Dear Henrie,

I am retiring from farm life. I don't want to live down here anymore. I want to move near my friends. I can live very comfortably and have even bought a small place near Carey in the new development on 48 (George and Carey's old farm). They call it Walnut Acres. You remember all of the walnut trees in their woods? I want you to come back and take over the farm. I don't have any need for money. Pap's building business left me better off than we were when he was alive. He worked hard all his life, and now I don't have to worry at all. But I don't want to sell the farm and see it turned into Blackberry Acres or something. I don't think I could stand that. I want you to have it. I want you to find a good man like Pap, who will work hard and help you. I don't have any chickens here now, except my new pet. I named her Cecilia. She is nice company when I am out in the yard, hanging out wash, or when I am working in the garden. The garden keeps getting smaller and smaller.

I don't seem to be able to take care of as much anymore. Tony the Tiger has died too. I had to put him to sleep. Everybody here is getting too old. Cecilia is constantly on the move and setting a good example for me to keep getting around too. Maybe when I move in near Carey, I'll look for another Tony to sit in my lap while I string beans or roll my hair at night. Henrie, please come back. I want you to have a chance at a happy, settled life. People need family near them. The farm will be all yours. You can do what you want with it. Even sell a little of it. But I don't think that would be necessary. I can help you with money to get started. All of the fields are leased out now. If you want to change that, you could. In other words, it would be yours to do with as you see. I wouldn't interfere. I just want to see you happy in your life.

Please come home.

Grandma

This was just what Henrie had been fighting to keep from admitting before, the pain of separation and the need for her grandmother's presence. At least she could face the request from a little hill of victory now. What was she thinking? She had less now than she had yesterday morning! But she felt like she had more! She didn't know what more that was, but when she lifted the covers on Nate's bed last night to have him crawl in next to her, both still warm from their showers, she hadn't been thinking anything, except that maybe she could have one last night of fun in her life. She hadn't been ready for what happened though. It was disappointing for the briefest part of a moment before she succumbed to some part of her that wanted him for more than what she wanted him to do.

She suddenly saw a place in life where the landscape was like a calm lake, flat, and where other parts of life could reflect; where the rise and fall of the sun made waves of mysterious color, and where clouds passing over threw shadows. Surrounding the still lake were mountains, holding everything in.

The ring of mountains was the freedom of security and the constant steadiness of something, like caring; maybe love.

Henrietta could only hold Nate and tell him she didn't care. She suddenly didn't care that things could be hard. With him on her, she felt Rubenesque.

It wasn't long after that, she realized he was asleep. She still wanted to hold him to her, and to feel his tight body in her arms. Then she had an image as she fell asleep, in that twilight place in her mind, of herself as the ring of mountains around Nate's valley.

The very next thing, Nate was pushing against her chest and stomach. He was really hurting her. All feelings of safety flew screaming from her mind. She panicked for a moment and yelled his name. She thought she had gotten into bed with some kind of maniac. Then she realized that Nate was just having a dream. She grabbed him and held him down to her. She got him to lie still while she untangled the bedcovers.

Whatever had stopped Nate the night before had gone from his mind by the morning. The strangest thing happened when they were making love, with the hot morning sun burning on them through the window. She thought she could smell that familiar, warm, winter-kitchen smell you get when you're cleaning chickens. Down at the bottom of the feathers, near the skin, there's the odor of just-released life. She could swear she smelled the bedroom too, downstairs at home. When it was raining outside in the fall, just almost to be winter, the bed would be cool in the afternoon gray as she lay on it, watching raindrops roll down the glass of the window and off the lower leaves of the big oak tree outside.

Things that get planted at that age, in the time of the soul's open furrows, can take years to germinate. Henrie felt she was finally beginning to germinate now, so many years later.

When Nate was fighting back awake after dozing from their lovemaking, he startled her from her own new sleep. But she was ready that time to grab him, in calm control. She was surprised that he was only anxious about being late for work.

Henrietta had come to assume that nobody worked. At least nobody in the hotel. She was more pleasantly surprised when he got dressed and grabbed a carpenter's belt out of the closet and stood over her, with it hanging heavy in his hand. She was shy in front of him and didn't want to let him see her naked. Just after he left, she could only think of Pap, lying in bed sick again and Grandma constantly carrying things up to him while his study sat idle, plans still weighted open on the table.

For some unknowable reason, maybe a stack of reasons, she suddenly felt it would be right for her to go back. If Nate wanted to go too, he could. There was very little doubt in her mind. Henrie was realizing that the mind knew things it wouldn't tell you until you were ready for them. That sounded sort of silly; like you had one mind outside of you, and another inside of you. But it seemed true to her. Some part of her had known that this was coming all along, and that part had been waiting for the rest of her to learn it, too.

Well...? She almost wanted to just sit for a while and see if anything else would come to her. But she had to pack her things and get them over to Nathan's room before Benny came up. She didn't even know if he would let them both stay in one room. But there was no reason to tell Benny. Let him find out on his own. Goddam pervert.

<h1 style="text-align:center">twenty-seven</h1>

Nate had run out of the hotel, swinging his heavy tool belt in his hand, happy in the bright sun. He had talked himself into believing that Nancy and Danson wouldn't notice him coming in late. He could only think of the freedom of Henrietta's strawberry body.

He moved lightly up the last half-block of Shotwell, warm and contented. Nate stepped from the bright sun, through the back room double doors, and into the low-ceilinged woodshop. "Good morning, Bob!"

Bob didn't want to look up from the table saw as Nate threaded his way through the machines and across to the order boxes.

"Hey, Bob!" Nate was more insistent. "How you doing this morning?" Nate stopped to put on his tool belt. He was a sturdy horse slipping back into a well-fitted harness. He turned around to pull the orders from his box. His name tag was missing. He half-turned back to Bob, but then leaned down and peeked into the box opening. There were no orders inside. Nate twisted his head around, looking over his outreached arm. Bob was setting the saw extremely carefully, his head down close to the table. Nate was puzzled for a moment.

"I told you, you don't work here anymore, so don't look for job orders."

Nate yanked his head around. There was Danson, predatory, in the doorway from the front office.

"Let's go, " Danson said, turning. "You can get your check up front."

There was no chance for Nate to say anything. He didn't move immediately to follow but looked back at Bob, who was now going into one of his coughing fits. Laughing and coughing were the same thing coming from Bob. Too many years of breathing the wood dust. Bob wasn't laughing now. He was coughing up a goodbye.

Nate had often imagined himself one day sitting in a chair beside Bob's bed in the scrubby little house up on Nevada Street, with Big Jack lying on the bed next to Bob, nuzzling his cold nose at Bob's hand. "Fuck it, Nate," Bob would say. "I'm a dead man anyway. Besides, I always liked the taste of sawdust, ever since I was a little kid. Fuck it, man. Don't worry about it."

If Nate had had the anger he wanted he could have pulled the hammer out of his belt and sailed it across the shop, right through that fresh stack of leaning windows at the back. The crashing rattle of the sawdusted panes would have satisfied him.

He didn't though. He pictured letting the hammer go, and the throw could be off, crooked. It could hit Bob and knock him onto the now-singing table saw. Nate already had blood on his hands. He was covered in blood. Nate turned while Bob coughed out his goodbye, keeping his head down over the saw.

In the hall, Danson waited, lit in silhouette, taller and wider than Nate usually thought of him. When Nate stepped into the hall, Danson wheeled again to march out to the front, without a word.

The ass of Danson's pants was shiny, and his brown western shirt bunched out in the back. Danson's skull was bald on the top, a bright orb Nate followed. Nate's hammer hand itched to pop a nice clean impression, about the size of a quarter, in that glistening pate.

Danson pushed through the swinging door and they passed his cluttered office, emerging into the sunny sales room. Nancy stood behind the counter, her whole body pouting at the cheap, wood-paneled room.

It could have been the way her teeth fought with her upper lip for freedom; or her breasts thrust forward over the desk; something neutralized Nate in her presence. Maybe it was those dark eyes she threw on him like she was sure that he wanted her.

Two men were in the corner of the showroom, at the windows, where the southern sun was pouring in. Nate recognized the applications they were filling out. "Don't waste any fucking time do you, Danson?"

He snapped around to Nate. "Shut up, Ring. I told you not to come back here after Friday night. If I have any trouble with you, I'll call the police."

Nate's head buzzed suddenly. What the fuck was Danson talking about? Nate pulled his head back into his shoulders. They had had another argument about the "Frisco Special" windows. Danson didn't tell him never to come back to work! Nate knew what was happening around him. He always made sure he knew. It was imperative that he always knew. He would never allow himself, he would never be, his mother.

Danson was just a shit-sucking...shit. All he did was suck out of the business, never putting anything back. The shop was falling apart, but he had just bought Nancy a new condo, and himself a new car. And every night they went out to some fancy place to eat, and always came in the next morning to excitedly tell Bob about where they had been, and what they had eaten. Danson was sucking the life out of the business, and out of Bob. He'd never get a chance to suck the life out of Nate. He'd have to hire some new asshole desperate enough to work for him.

"Make out Mr. Ring's check." Danson threw the verbal order at Nancy as he ducked back into his office.

Nate let his boots stomp across the squeaking old wood floor, ignoring the applicants now. Nancy sat behind the sales counter. Nate leaned and his hammer knocked loudly against the wooden counter between them. She wouldn't look up at him. Nancy's hair was black, curled up on her head, short. Her eyes had blue shadow on them, smeared deeply. Nate watched her look down as she threaded the check into her typewriter. Her face moved as if she were concentrating all she had on this task. Her breasts inside the gray sweater almost touched her hands as she typed. Her lips moved as she typed his name. Nate wanted to put a bloody kiss on Nancy's unruly lips. He looked down at himself as if he would suddenly see blood all over his clothes.

He followed the clacking of Nancy's typewriter as it pecked out his name, NATHAN RING, and then the numbers on his check, and then a string of XXXXX's.

Nate was awake from the bear dream, all wrapped in the blankets, trapped with Henrietta. He hadn't even known he was punching into her stomach, trying to get up and out of the covers.

"Nate. Nate! You're hurting me!"

He had to lie there, claustrophobic, his mind a little frantic while Henrietta tugged the blankets from under herself. As she made soft, sweet struggling sounds and rolled side to side, he could feel her breasts and thighs rubbing against him. He began to grow hard between her legs. Her complexion flushed as her eyes met his and then looked slightly away. He was reminded of the complexion of a peach or some fruit. He put his arms around her in the loosening blanket. He wanted to screw the way they would have if they inhabited another time in human history, maybe between animal skins or rolling in the dirt. Free.

In the dream he was having when he woke up, his cabbie pulled them into the dark courtyard of a wide low building in the half-moon light of a Mexican night. The air was tropical and still. Climbing out of the car he could hear twittering voices, like birds singing jungle songs. He moved toward the low front of the house, a grand adobe, spread out. The double doors suddenly swung open and singing women poured out to him. All of them were dressed in diaphanous robes as colorful as the jungle birds they imitated, and they surged toward Nate his roommate from LA, Pete, surrounding them. He felt like a swaying forest branch where flights of luxurious color swarm down to an undulating rest, their song caressing him: "Pick me. Pick me. Pick me."

Nate was unnerved, shot through with their electricity. His eyes tried to single out the faces of individual women, but his senses weren't clear at all. Someone grabbed him by the arm, with pleasant cool hands. He was thankful for the rooting steadiness. He looked down. She had short curly hair, dark, and dark eyes, and bright lips pushed out a little by her teeth. He could see the other girls now. All had dark hair and dark skin; Hispanic, Chinese, Northern European, or Japanese, or African. He had no chance to completely identify any of them before he was swept to the house by the girl who held his arm.

She led him through the wide doors into a large, low-ceilinged room lit by glowing lanterns and candles. It was just dim enough so you couldn't see anything clearly.

Every time he looked at her, she seemed more incongruous. Her skin was from a woman with much lighter hair. For a strange second, he thought her eyes reflected the candlelight a fancy green, and he thought her lips were pale, rosy. He almost thought he saw a dark spot on her lower lip.

He looked around them. All the women had taken on various shades of gold in this light. She held him captive in her rosy, golden, chiffon-flowing grasp.

The other girls wandered away as if he had been spoken for. She and Nate were left alone near the doors. She held tight to his arm.

Nate noticed a sunken area toward the back of the room. He blinked to focus his unbelieving eyes. He saw a bear down there, hunched down. The bear was immobile, maybe stuffed, looking bored or a little depressed. Nate couldn't see any chains or restricting ropes. The sunken floor wasn't deep enough to be a prison. Nate stepped forward to see the bear better. Was he alive? Was it a she? The bear was unresponsive. The girl reached out and pulled Nate back to her. She took his chin in her warm fingers. She pulled his face to her, almost as if she were jealous of the bear. Nate didn't mind. She peeled her lips open like a peach. She pulled Nate down to her. He eagerly pressed his tongue into the fresh fruit.

After no more than a moment of letting him taste her ripe mouth, she pulled back again, reluctantly, and stepped back.

"Would you like to go to my room?" She squeezed his arm tightly in her hand.

Nate could only whisper "yes" from a dry throat.

She pulled his ear down to her lips and sounded coquettish. "They will want you to dance with the bear first."

Nate stepped back to look at her. Her voice still tickled in his ear canal. Dance with the bear? Suddenly Nate wanted to laugh, one of those bending-over gut laughs that takes over everything. Her face had a little girl's look of almost comic seriousness. Dance with the bear? What? Dance with the bear to get into bed with the girl. Nate put his arm around her small shoulders. He let it slide down the smooth fabric of her robe, to her waist, and then to her butt. He could feel her firm sloping skin slip back and forth beneath the fabric. He could dance with the bear. Sure. Certainly, with one that looked as bored, almost dead, as this one. He shook his head quietly. She smiled brightly with her incongruously colored luscious lips. She pulled his face down to taste the peach again. That was enough for Nate. He spun and headed for the dance area. The floor beneath him was flagstone. The dancing pit, down four steps, had been polished to a perfect slickness.

All of the other girls and Pete, expectant, gathered to the middle of the room, away from their couches and card games. Quiet bird music floated around him again. As Nate neared, the bear perked up his head. Did they make this demand of every customer? Probably, if only to see what kind of foolish suckers would fall for it. But especially when business was off and they needed to be entertained. Well, they were going to be entertained. If this was the price, Nate remembered the broken-skin peach of her mouth. He stopped next to the bear and put his right hand on its unhappy back, as if to say "hello" to an old friend, familiar. Nate dropped his left hand down in an invitation to dance. The bear, with no sigh of enthusiasm, began to move, to stretch up, until he, it was a 'he,' was standing over the surprised Nate by well more than a foot. Nate would have to reach his arm around the bear's heavy body to hold on.

The bear's face looked to have been cut from stone. It was immobile. His fur was stiff and warm. From somewhere in the back of the room came music that sounded faintly Latin and faintly like something that would have been popular in the fifties. Was it music that the bear had requested? After a few stumbling starts the bear began to follow Nate's lead. The girl with Pete began clapping and all of their voices were alive again. Nate led the bear so that he could keep his own girl in view. She was standing quietly at the edge of the higher floor. Her face carried no emotion. Nate could still taste her fruity lips. He turned back and pulled down on the bear's right arm, to put a dip and glide into the next step. Heavily, and without warning, the bear's arm popped out of his body. Nate grasped at it, cumbersome, shocked. The upper part of the arm thumped and dragged on the floor. The hole in the shoulder immediately began to spurt blood. Nate stopped dancing. It had to be some kind of joke. He waited for the laughs of entertainment behind him. They didn't come. He twisted to look around the room. Suddenly, the other arm fell out on its own, hitting the floor with a bone-thumping clunk. Blood spurted in a stream over Nate's shoulder. As he whipped back, the bear's head rolled off its body and dropped to the floor like a sickening, loud cabbage. Its neck drenched Nate in a geyser of slick blood. He let go of the bear's body. Not out of horror, but surprise. It stood by itself, a gruesome fountain. Nate stepped quickly back, and slipped in the blood, flopping onto the slick dancing floor. Scrambling, he fought his way to his feet. With his arms arched protectively over his head he slipped and fell again. He twisted around to see the girl. She was still. She seemed to want to move but couldn't. She called encouragement, but Nate couldn't hear her. His hands and knees slipped in the thickening blood. Then, as if the fountain had spent itself, it suddenly fell, crushing him to the floor under its mountainous weight. He couldn't breathe. He was frantic. Where was she? She was the one he was doing this for, and she was crying for him, and for her frustration. Nate's heart tried to leap out of him in a howl, like a cub for its mother, or a wolf for its mate. He choked. It was too deep. He couldn't bring it up.

Out of breath, Nate could hear his name being called. He was suffocating. He freed his left hand and pushed up. The slick hard floor went soft under him, and on top of him the bear was interminably heavy.

"Nate! Stop it! You're hurting me!"

His eyes yanked open like a slap. He was shoving his fist into Henrietta's stomach. It was terrifying how tangled they had become in each other, wrapped in the blankets. She pulled him down, tight against her, until he stopped moving. But then she started moving under him with such grace and softness, trying to untangle them, that he felt himself being drawn into the safety of her home.

"Would you sign this for me Mr. Danson?"

Danson had come back out of the office and was rustling behind Nancy, looking into the order file for something. His shirt tail was still hanging sloppily out of the back of his pants.

Nate pretended the game of their working relationship was real. Nancy stood, her butt poking out behind her as if at some kind of attention, waiting for Danson to sign the check.

When she turned back with the signed check, she wouldn't let her eyes rest on Nate. She lifted them past him to the men in the windows and pushed the check across the counter.

Nate held back any "thank you". He turned slowly to the door. One of the men started toward the desk. He was in his mid-forties. His face was red and puffy, like an alcoholic's. Nate could feel, in the way the man ignored him and smiled ingratiatingly toward Nancy, the frightening, desperate need for work.

Nate had a stupid sense of freedom as he stepped out into the sunshine of October. He did need some way of taking care of Henrietta. She didn't have anything.

He shook his head at himself when he realized what he was thinking. He had already made her a part of him. Was it Nate and Henrietta, Henrietta and Nate, in his mind now?

twenty-eight

The metal hardware on Henrietta's suitcase was trying to reshape the bones in Nate's ass. He sat in his room, listening to her. He had forgotten to take off his carpenter's belt after leaving the shop, a little in shock. The belt felt like a protective truss. He wanted to stand up. "Henrie" her grandmother called her. "It's spelled R I E Nate." He didn't want to concentrate on what Henrie was reading. He was staring at his floor, trying to discern which of the blotches were part of the linoleum and which had come later. He missed a lot of the letter as he thought back on it. He wouldn't ever be able to remember the words later, but he knew what they meant right now. That much was clear.

Lucky, nothing real had passed between them. Nothing. She hadn't given him anything that she would have to take back. There had been no real reason to expect that losing his job would affect her. If he was he, standing near the edge of the road, at the edge of Monastery Beach, and Mona was getting on her bicycle to ride away, there would have been no comparison. There was nothing even remotely similar. There was no reason to feel that a man's new, or even his old, or even some ancient, memory of freedom could be threatened.

In his imagination, Nate got up from her suitcase and walked to his window and stood there looking out. As he imagined he watched the street, he imagined he pulled the hammer out of his belt; and, like some TV cowboy, he twirled it in the air and caught it. In his mind, he threw it up again, to catch it twirling again as it fell. The beauty of the stunt was the feel in your hand when it hit right. It wasn't anything that could be shared. It just felt good. Nate knew Henrietta had stopped reading the letter. He heard her fold the loud pieces of blue paper. He wanted to feel the sharp push of an uncontrollable set of protruding front teeth against his lips. He wanted to feel Nancy turn and push her butt against him.

"Would you like to come to Ohio sometime?"

He laughed inside himself somewhere and could almost feel his belt move with the muscles, squeezing him as he sat uncomfortably on the suitcase. Would he like to come to Ohio sometime? You mean kind of like falling out of an airplane as it was flying over low and slow? Or like riding a bus through and being thrown off in the middle of the road in the middle of the night? Or do you mean something like knocking on the door to an empty house somewhere, waiting until nobody answers?

Nate lifted his shoulders in a shrug and dropped his head down a little further between his arms, to study the floor. He was right about the floor. More than half of the pattern there was not original.

"You would have a place to stay anytime you want to come." He started to move his lips but didn't. Then he did. He spoke. "Good. You mean I can have a cot on the back porch?"

Shit! Why did he say that? What he got was what he was gonna get. He had no right to expect more. He couldn't keep his head down or she would know what he was thinking.

"That's good, Henrie." What the hell was he calling her that for? "I'm glad for you." He finally did look up at her face. It hung a tiny bit sideways, like she wanted to see him from another angle. He wanted to see himself from another angle too. He wanted to see the whole goddam world from another angle.

There was a sudden sadness in her eyes. No. It was confusion, disappointment. Nate had shoved the conversation off on an oblique angle.

She didn't know why Nate was acting like this. Honestly, he was being an asshole. She had thought he would be happy about it. All he did was sit there, with his head down between his arms, staring at the floor, like some lost little boy, hiding his feelings from everybody.

"Nate, I don't know how you're going to take this." Henrietta's voice was not what she wanted it to be. It sounded a little impatient to her. She tried to back up in her mind. He still had his head down between his arms. Moment by moment, she could see the tiniest little movement, of his eyelash as he blinked, of his lips as he breathed in or out. He was listening to her. "I wouldn't even be reading this letter if it weren't for you."

There was a burning in the back of his nose.

"Nate." In a way this kind of pissed her off. Why was he making her work so hard for it? Did she have to spell everything out for him? Would she always have to spell everything out for him? "Nate. Would you want to come with me?"

"You mean for a visit?" He almost sniffled. He pressed his elbows down hard into his legs.

"Well. If that's what you want. You could come and stay too. If you wanted."

"Do you know why I'm back from work so early?"

"No. It isn't lunchtime already?"

Jesus! Nate sniffed. He half-laughed, to cover the noise of his nose. "No." He half-laughed again, as he said it. "No. It's because I got fired." He looked up at Henrietta now. He thought he had himself under control. She was smiling curiously at him, trying to keep track of what was going on with his odd laughs.

Henrietta saw Nate's red eyes. He had been crying. But now he was laughing. The crying part was the important one. Was he crying because he was going to lose her? Or was he crying because she wanted him to go with her?

freedom

twenty-nine

A sudden tearing roar slammed past Nate's window. As suddenly as it hit him the roar was gone, leaving only the steady echo of two trains passing in the night in the desert. Impatience with wakefulness and the noisy interruptions of his memories made Nate childishly irritable with his rolling prison.

"What was that Nate?"

He turned back to Henrietta. Her eyes were partially open. The sleepiness of her mouth made him ache to be somewhere else with her, holding her close, keeping a different rocking vigil with the dark night.

"Just another train passing." He said quietly. "Going the other way." He swung back quickly as the last roaring car flew by the window and left a chopping emptiness of receding sound. He started to say, "You don't know how fast you're going until...", but she had fallen asleep again. Nate turned back to his window and looked up, to try and find the missing moon. The desert, if that's where they were, was black and empty.

. . .

Nate edged toward the cop, like some kind of calf or lamb testing the limits of the fenced field. He stopped and stood back from the cop. The fat man came out of his cubicle, looking toward the policeman, trying to gain approval for trying to be helpful. He didn't look at Nate. Nate watched another cop help the man to the front door and out through the complicated lock. Nate turned back and could see Henrietta in her cubicle, looking up at him from writing something. He could tell she could tell he was in some kind of trouble.

Nate's policeman led him gently by the arm into the fat man's empty cubicle, near the back door. The soft carpeted walls of the movable partition immediately began to soak up noise. It was close and quiet in the tiny space. The steel-framed chair, though it had a cushioned seat, didn't comfort Nate.

■　■　■

There wasn't any kind of joke he could tell these penis lips jokers that would take their mind off taking him back to his Dad. They listened more to the scratching squawk of their goddam radio than they would to some twelve-year-old pissant. They didn't care if he got beat up when they left him. The plastic seat was cold if he moved even a tiny bit off the spot in the middle, where his ass had finally gotten it warm. The heat from the front of the car where those shitheads sat couldn't cut through his freezing jacket. Who the fuck told them to look for him under Helen's porch? Some shit-lips fingered him. If he jumped out of the car to run, he knew he'd be a plugged turd. All it took was one second of thinking that this situation wasn't as serious as these fuckers with the guns thought it was.

■　■　■

"Okay fella." The cop was talking low in the quiet booth. Like a confession booth. "I'd like you to fill out this form, just the way you remember things.

I need you to write it out yourself, in your own writing. As you can read at the top of this sheet here, you have the right to remain silent, and anything you say can be used against you in a court of law. You have the right to have an attorney with you during questioning, and if you can't afford one, you're entitled to have the court appoint one."

A lizard of fear scrambled up Nate's back. What the shit was going on? "Am I being arrested?" That unmistakable constriction grabbed his throat. He wondered what was in his voice.

"No. You're not being arrested. But I do need to have a statement that is as truthful as you remember it. We're taking statements from everybody so we can find out what really happened out there."

"Why do I feel nervous then? Something makes me wonder what that other guy said to you."

"Now, don't worry about what the other people are saying. Just write it down exactly the way you remember it."

What were they going to do? Take him out against the driveway wall and shoot him if he didn't fill out the damn paper? Henrietta was in her booth, filling hers out; diligently and efficiently probably. This bullshit was not part of Nate's world. These people weren't a part of what happened. Why weren't they there for the real trouble? They just came around afterward to point the finger at somebody. It was too easy for things to get all unstuck in their hands.

The blood on Nate's hands was dried. He knew it could be his blood as easy as anyone else's. He could be flopped out on the cold linoleum floor, spitting viscous red spit, trying to get the cop's shoes, trying to leave a stain of his life on them. Maria would come back and jump over to him and pick his bloody head up in her arms, and poor Henrietta would leap out of her cubicle, yelling at the bastards. She would push the little girl out of the way and try to do something to help him. He didn't know what, but she would do something to try to fix him up, to bring him back to life. A hopeless cause.

The cop went to get coffee for himself and Manini, who was in the next tiny cubicle talking to Henrietta in low tones. Nate put his head down on the paper and tried to hold his eyes closed. Someone threw a bucket of black liquid at him. It splattered his skin, searing him. No. It wasn't searing. It melted his skin in one quick moment. Whoever was standing next to Nate was screaming. He couldn't lower his head to see himself. He turned to the man screaming next to him. His skin was melting off under the strange blueness of the street corner light. A black and white car was speeding away, laughing. Nate tried to shake himself. The hooks of the dream were in his skin.

"Mr. Ring! You have to fill out the form. You can't go to sleep! What do you think this is? Now come on!" The cop pulled noisily on a chair as if to sit, but instead stood next to Nate. "We need you to start with your name and your contact details there at the top of the form. And could I see your ID, driver's license, or other state-issued ID?"

At that moment, another female voice entered the space accompanied by what sounded like another cop, telling her to take a seat. Nate barely eyeballed out there and saw there were two people, a young guy about thirty or so, in the process of pulling Nate's previous chair under him. He had nearly white-blond hair and his face was brushed with a thin red beard. He heard a woman's voice and peeked around the cop and saw her, her crisp yellow shirt under an open grey tweed jacket. She was well-pressed, and casual, but still tucked and pulled together. Her curly hair was almost monolithic, like the matted ears of a poodle. Her face had dark freckles sprinkled on it. She was also in the process of scraping a chair on the linoleum and sitting. Another cop moved in behind them once they were sitting, almost between them, favoring the woman.

Nate's policeman crowded Nate's small space. "Sir, may I see your ID please?" he said, with the slightest exasperation in his voice. Nate reached for his wallet and pulled out his driver's license and his San Francisco Public Library card and laid them gently smoothed out on the table like they wanted to sleep there. The cop eyed the library card and pushed it back, then picked up the license and began to peruse it. Nate peeked out and the woman and man were half-pointing at him. Here it was, a certain, crushing example of the future. What Nate feared was the future. The future? The future was arriving every moment; in bits and pieces, in chunks; in fucking landslides. The future was now. But that was too abstract. He feared the loss of freedom now; or even worse, in the time that was coming toward him, dusting in roaring tumbles. He could almost feel his body ready to coil as if to leap out of the way of a landslide. But it could not fully coil. He could not muster the leap and the run. The only protection he had was to hide his head and let the tumble roll over his back, bouncing over him or crushing him, finally freeing him. While the cop noted his information from the card on the top of the form, Nate put his head back down on his arms.

Fuck them. Really, just fuck them. They could figure out what happened without him. What he needed was sleep. Half in his mind, he could tell that the policeman had turned and left, exasperated. He was now talking to Henrietta and the other cop. He heard what he thought was the woman's voice at the table say something like "No, he was trying to save the man from himself...." He heard something like a "Hmm," or "Uh hunh...." or the like from a man. Then, from nearer, Nate heard somebody, in a whisper he thought was Henrietta, say something like, "stock," or probably "shock." He didn't have the strength to lift his head and ask what kind of "shock, and who it was they were talking about."

Of course, he was in shock. It was him they were talking about. He wanted to be thrown across the room, to feel life, but all he could feel was the landslide of the future bearing down on him and he wanted to be somewhere fucking else when he opened his eyes.

"Nate?"

Okay. He didn't know what he would see when he lifted his head, but he would give them this chance. Through his arms that were hanging a little off the edge of the desk in the cubicle, he could see that it was still indeed bright in the room. He blinked his eyes and almost laughed to himself. Maybe he did win this time. Maybe, before kids were forced into growing up, whatever shape the world had in their imaginations, was the shape it truly had. Nate lifted his eyes a little and they started to adjust to the light in the room. He was afraid of what he would see. Were those two new people from the loony bin? They could be waiting quietly, just like they had for his mom, surrounding her almost, making it certain she could not escape. If so, he'd just put his head back down. What fucking difference would that make? They could come to any conclusion they wanted. He would just call in absent.

Only it was Henrietta standing near him. She had moved so close that she blocked his vision of anything else in the room. Her fingers lightly touched his shoulder. He raised his head higher and could see that she had tried to clean off her blouse some. He must have been sleeping. Her blouse was clinging, wet. He wanted to lift his head and push it into her and hold it there. He wanted HER to lift his head and pull it into her and hold it there. As if that was all she wanted at all.

"We can go, Nate. They said that the statements of the witnesses, including mine, are enough to let you go. We can go now."

He turned up to her face. No one was standing over her shoulder. She was probably telling the truth. He couldn't see any white-coated mental health wardens behind her. Had he really expected to see them? He didn't know what he expected, but he hadn't let them control him. He had shown that it was possible to win, that it was possible to live outside the law.

thirty

Some dreams are distortions of present events or desires or even nicer arrangements of facts. Sometimes they are merely records of reality, like stored accounts that return to be played again. Henrietta had dreams like these, very prosaic accounts of events. It was almost as if she needed another look to see properly all that had happened. She trusted her dream memory to keep things straight. She trusted it to store and retrieve events clearly and effortlessly. No matter what she had gone through, she didn't have the complicated nightmares some people talked about. She had never been afraid to go to sleep because of what she might dream. There had been times when she was afraid to go to sleep, like in the hotel, because of what could really happen to her. But she wasn't afraid of dreams.

She had no trouble falling asleep on the train. She knew where she was going now. She knew what would be there. She knew the life that was waiting for her already. She had few trepidations, and those little ones wouldn't keep her awake.

Why hadn't Henrietta been surprised at Grandma's letter, when she stopped packing for the move into Nate's room and sat down on the edge of her bed to read it? Why had she been afraid to read it before? Henrie wasn't even surprised that Grandma offered her the farm. What had always before been the men's place to do had now become the women's; holding land and passing it down, trying to keep it in the family. If Henrietta got married, who would the farm pass down to? The name she had adopted back into would change. Felix, Pap's name would be gone. Well, at least some of the blood would be the same; diluted a lot now from Pap and Grandma, down through her mother, diluted by her father. Who would dilute it with her? Would it really be diluting it?

Would it be Nathan? She didn't know if Nate would even have the guts to marry her. He was the skittish sort.

These were strange things for her to be thinking about. It was like they were given to her as her place to think about. But she wasn't ready yet—for the, somehow to her, masculine feel of it. It seemed hard to get men to live as long as women did nowadays. They seemed able to get only so far before they keeled over. Maybe it was from too much work. But it wasn't that the women didn't work. They just seemed able to take it better.

thirty-one

The bumps under Henrie's eyelids reminded Nate of someone's hand playing games under a blanket, running back and forth, not wanting to sleep. He touched each of her eyes lightly more than once when she was asleep. And he remembered an old song by Richie Havens, about "two hearts dreaming as one." Nate wished he could dream with her.

Tommy seemed to have big dreams for Nate and Henrietta. Nate wished he could have seen inside Tommy's mind. Maybe he could have persuaded him to come with them. Tommy should have dreams of his own.

Nate sat next to the head of Tommy's bed like he had almost every day for a week. He had come to visit with Tommy. Henrietta came just to be with Nate.

"Tommy?" Nate asked and turned to Henrietta for approval. "We've been talking...and we want you to come with us, back to Ohio. Henrie and I want you to live with us."

It was strange, the way Tommy sat there for a minute, totally quiet. First, he looked at Henrietta. He knew that the invitation was real. Tommy moved his eyes back to the TV. It always seemed to be running at low volume, sitting on the dresser by the window. He didn't seem to want to look at Nate.

Tommy suddenly pushed off the bed. He shuffled across the room in his stocking feet. He started changing the channels as if he hadn't heard any questions. His shirt hung like a flour sack thrown over a scarecrow's frame. The bandage was a sad lump at his waist. Tommy held himself as straight as possible.

If he had been younger, Nate thought, Tommy would have jumped back to his former self this week. But he hadn't seemed to want to jump back. In a matter of seconds now, with Henrie here, he was almost recovered. Nate glanced at Henrietta. She didn't understand what was going on. Her eyes were on him.

Now, Tommy was shoving the conversation off in another direction. Just like Nate had when Henrie had asked him to go with her. Was this just something men did? Tommy resolutely clicked the knob around until he had looked at all of the channels, and then he ended again with the first one. Tommy had relied on Nate to change the channels when they were alone. He hadn't seemed to mind lying in bed, talking to Nate over a ball game, or over a game show, about how exciting Ohio was going to be for Nate. When he wanted the channel changed he let Nate do it. He let Nate help him down to the T&M a couple of times for lunch, and once out for burritos. Nate even ran down and brought food up to him; chimichangas and pupusas. Now, Tommy was suddenly able to do everything for himself. Nate stared at the floor again. He looked back up to Henrie. She sat quietly straight, her hands still in her lap. Her face seemed concerned, but she was going to take all directions from him. "So, what do you think Tommy?" Henrietta blinked as she heard Nate's voice again.

Tommy turned half around from the TV as if he had been engrossed in it. "It's an okay show."

This time Nate couldn't control his exasperation. He showed his face to Henrietta. "What the hell do you think about going to Ohio with us?"

Tommy walked back to the bed quietly. He sat on the edge, not allowing any sign or hint of pain show on his face. His hair hung over his forehead. Its whiteness contrasted with his sun-darkened skin. Nate watched Tommy's face intently.

Tommy turned away to Henrietta. "I don't know why I would want to go."

It pissed Nate off that Tommy wouldn't look at him. "Because you can be with friends then. We can all live together. There's plenty of room. It's a big house. You can cook if you want. And Henrie and I can raise chickens and I'll do some carpentry."

Tommy kept looking at Henrietta for a minute, then shook his head and swung back to the TV again, blankly staring at it.

Henrie obviously wished she could help Nate.

"Tommy! Why not? It's a perfect match." Nate had reached vocal exasperation.

Tommy pushed up from the bed again and walked toward the TV. He stopped, blocking Nate's view of Henrietta. Nate wanted some sign of what was going on. They obviously knew, but why didn't he? Tommy snapped off the TV and swung around to face Nate. "I don't have any need to go to some farm in Ohio."

Nate could only look back down to the floor to try to find anything that made sense.

Tommy leaned down, holding onto the dresser, to pull his rubber-bottom cotton shoes on one by one. If it hurt, and Nate was certain it did, Tommy didn't allow it to show on his face. When he was through, he took a few steps toward the door. "Let's go down to the T&M and have some coffee. I need to see something different."

Nate stared back down at the floor, not moving for a moment. He could hear Henrie get up from her chair and push it back under the window. Nate was going to have to get up too. They seemed to have things figured out better than he did. Everybody always did.

They sat at one of the tables in the T&M's front window, Nate near the glass. Henrie put her hand on Nate's arm. He had to look away, out to the street. Outside the window, people were streaming by on a late Tuesday afternoon. Suddenly, part of the stream stopped. A little black kid, probably about five, holding his mother's hand, was led over by the window. Nate didn't even look up to see the mother. She was wearing a white knitted dress that fit her thin shape nicely. The kid leaned sideways against the window, impatient, while his mother bent down to tie his shoe. The little boy's eyes found Nate and were glued on him. Something about the shape of the boy's head captured Nate's attention. The boy's skin was clear brown. His forehead was smooth, rounded. His hair was short, tight wired. His black eyes first looked at Nate as they might at something strange, like staring into a cage at the zoo. Nate was fascinated by the clear curious sorrow in the dark eyes. No, it wasn't sorrow. Just some human need to reach out to the world and know more. It was as if both were transfixed. The boy's mother: slim, neat, and organized, her hair shaped like a stiff drape over her head, stood back up. Seeing her son's gaze consumed, she looked in at Nate, then over to Henrietta. Her face was small. Her features were thin-swept. Something like wonder washed quickly across them. She tried to control it, not wanting to show her obvious confusion about how anyone could sit, or eat in a cheap, dirty place like that. They moved away; the boy pulled along by his mother's fine, well-kept hand. When Nate turned back, Tommy was bringing them coffees on a tray. He was having trouble. Henrie grabbed Nate's arm when his chair scraped. "Let him do it." She said quietly.

The coffees had lost almost a third of their contents onto the tray, but no one mentioned it.

Nate knew how Henrietta had had to hammer at him to make him realize she wanted him with her. He would give it one more try. "Tommy. Henrie and I really want you to come with us. We're going to need help to get the place going again. Please come with us?"

Again, Tommy glanced at Henrietta before Nate. "Naw, Nate. I don't want to go. I don't want to live on some farm in Ohio. I couldn't stand to be that far from water. I belong here. I grew up here. I've lived most of my life here. I like it. Besides, this is something for you and Henrietta. It has nothing to do with me. I don't belong. I just happen to be somebody you met is all. You're going to have to do it on your own."

Nate's eyes weren't seeing Tommy. They weren't seeing anything very clearly. He had to put his head down. He felt Henrietta's hand on his leg as she squeezed it. Tommy wouldn't be going with them.

thirty-two

Looking out the train window, over the misty rock and pine slopes, Nate felt a wave through his body. Now, sleep had become construction and the waking hours in this mountain-slithering prison were deconstruction. Raindrops on the window stopped his vision, closing him tighter into his exhausted seat. Everything was disintegrating in his thoughts. The past and the future were fighting over him. He was the present, suspended like a bulging snake meal, waiting to be found indigestible and spit out into another life.

He hadn't been able to talk to Henrietta through all of their early railroad dinner. He wanted the freedom of someone like Tommy. He didn't want to completely sever from his past.

If he'd seen a girl that looked like Mona on the train—If he'd seen Mona on the train, he wouldn't have been able to grasp even one clear thought about it. He had no self now. He had only a frightened squeak of a chance for release from the constricting belly of the present.

Tommy let him know in plain words: "A man like you or me doesn't get very many chances for something good like your Henrietta. If you let her get away there won't be another chance coming.... You better listen to me because I'm not going to tell you more than one Goddam time." Tommy sat back against the pillows on his bed. If he made a grimace, Nate couldn't

175

see it because of the shadow the window shade cut across his face and chest. "This is the only thing I have left in the world to give you for a present Nate."

Nate was a little surprised. He half-expected Tommy to pull something out of the pocket of his soft jeans. "I know I've never given anybody anything worth having. When you move through water, you know, it closes right behind you. I haven't left any trail behind me. So if you can remember this, that will have to be my trail. Tommy leaned toward Nate who was sitting near the foot of the bed in a chair. The sun streaked across the lower part of Tommy's body, and across the old hand Tommy was pointing at him. His face had become visible again. "Don't EVER do anything to hurt Henrietta. If you do, you're a fool like me, boy. You don't want anyone else to go with you two. This is the chance of a lifetime. Believe me, boy, it doesn't matter so much what you do if it's the two of you doing it together."

"Do you hear me, Nate?" Tommy was still leaning forward. His face twisted in forceful meaning. "If you don't go to Ohio with her, alone, and do everything you can to keep her happy, then you're a bigger fool than me. At least you've got me to tell you from experience."

Nate felt suddenly cheap and foolish for thinking Tommy might have something in his pocket he wanted to give him.

Tommy started sounding angry. "If I was your age right now boy you wouldn't stand a chance with me. I'd have that girl off of you quicker than I used to slice the tips off the crew's steaks for me and the captain. You'd be standing there like a dumb swabbie!"

It pissed Nate off for Tommy to speak of Henrietta like she was just meat. Maybe it was good Tommy hadn't come. But he missed him. Nate wanted to turn his head and watch the moving hills through the rain, but he didn't. He would almost rather Henrietta think he was sleeping. That was all he really wanted anyway, was the freedom of deep and long sleep.

thirty-three

Entering the low door through the thick adobe wall Tommy was not going to church or going to a lonely late Saturday Mass.

He wasn't a tourist either, piling out of a bus the way they did a couple of times a day; to go shuffle through the old Mission and take photos and read the plaques set in the floor and then hurry on back to the souvenir shop before they were called to leave.

Tommy ducked quickly through the gift shop. He nodded his head briefly to the woman behind the case of trinket souvenirs. He passed the donation box by the door and stepped into the chapel.

Inside, Tommy stood under the small loft that jutted, old and wooden, out into the stucco room. He could feel the ancient air of the building. He could feel the ancient air of the people who had been there that morning, and mornings over a hundred years ago, at Mass and praying. Two thin bell ropes were strung down the back wall right next to him. A simple wooden grip hung on the end of each one. Tommy remembered the naive hopefulness of their ringing as he had heard them years before. They rang like young gongs beat from some scrap of metal off an abandoned ship.

Tommy preferred this chapel to the Basilica next door. That was someone else's idea of a church. Over there on Sunday, filled with a big congregation,

Tommy could grasp some of the meaning of a God above people, a powerful God. Alone, though, Tommy was always intimidated by the power, size, and grandeur of that building. The vaulting thrust of the heavenly-blue dome made him feel like he was being sucked up before his time. What Tommy liked about this old adobe chapel was that it felt like a working man's church; a church for little people. It had been built by working people. You could see the tool marks in the beams over the doors. You could run your hands over the hand-beaten iron gates that circled the baptismal font on the left and formed the communion railing at the front altar. The bright colors painted behind the altar statues and the chevrons painted on the ceiling were distinctive marks of the Spaniards and Indians who had built this church. If you moved up close to the side altars, you could see that they were carpentered by rough hands.

Tommy was no different from any of those ageless workmen. He was a little man in the world. He had no missionary significance. He was shepherded as much by the need of others' need to have a flock, as by his own need to be part of one.

Tommy didn't like the statue above the side altar, of the conquering Spanish missionary; sword in his right hand and a Bible in his left, held forward as if declaiming and fighting for God and enforcing God's word. He walked up the aisle, drawn without thought to the painting on the right wall, hung in a heavy rough-hewn frame. It was the Virgin Mary with the Christ Child. In the picture, the Virgin held the baby up and out, as if it were the fat baby of any mother, to show him off and offer him. The wrists and elbows and knees and ankles of the baby were lost in his fat. He had the dark hair and slightly flat face of a Spanish Indian baby. The Virgin had that tendency to roundness of many Spanish women. Her hair was dark and pulled back from her face, with ripples of curls across her head and down out of sight behind her shoulder. She wore a red robe with a deep, deep, blue mantle over it. Tommy stopped and knelt in the pew next to the painting. If he wanted to pray to anyone anymore, then it was to this woman. It was to this mother of healthy fat babies. Tommy looked down at his hands. He could see how old they were, papery, spotted. Luckily his work hadn't been the kind that left your hands beat up and sometimes missing parts. He'd spent his life handling soft fat cold meat, and butter and flour, in a steel room where cleanliness was a second religion. Tommy had spent his life safe and alone in his kitchen, with the cleanliness of his cold foods and the aching speed of the heat from his gas burners, making food for the working men. Those men might as well have been Chinese building a railroad, or the Indians building this Mission, or cowboys driving cows. They were only doing what they were told; given only small chances to have any more out of life than the solitude of their need to work and the necessary hunger at the end of the day.

In laying their section of rail, in the rise of a wall or the movement of cattle, in the passage of the nautical miles, they were nothing but fucking stiffs. But a Virgin like that, and a baby like that, were the chance for a difference. Tommy could see in his hands how old he truly was. It hadn't been too long ago when there was still possibility in him. He had spent his whole life emerging, but never emerged. He had stayed safe in the bud. Tommy had never loved anyone in his life more than himself. Not really. The only person he had come close with was Dolores, thirty-four years ago. But he had never given her more than it had been easy to give. He had always reserved the right, somewhere within himself, to be totally free. That was all he had ever wanted in life, was freedom. Well, he was completely free now. The Virgin in the painting was offering him the child, but he was much too old and much too free. Far too free.

thirty-four

As the train narrowed its aim, over switches and ever-slowing tracks, trying to find Denver, Henrietta sat with the side of her face against the back of the seat, watching the evening lights and ringing city crossings roll by. She also watched Nate fight to hold sleep. He'd been awake when she opened her eyes in Salt Lake City that morning. Nate didn't tell her he stayed awake all night, unable to sleep, but she knew. He didn't want her to realize how scared he was; of moving with her, living with her, of being in Ohio. He tried to get the only friend Henrietta knew of to move with them. He was scared out of his wits just being alone with her; afraid it wouldn't work and he'd be stuck on her farm in Ohio. She laughed to herself. If he was afraid of being alone with her, she wondered if he knew what that tiny valley was like in the winter, when it snowed good. You couldn't get out. If you weren't friends with the Hanes' at the next farm over then you wouldn't see anybody for a couple of days probably, except when the mailman drove his jeep up and honked and waved. Otherwise, you had to have your own jeep or wait until the county came along with the road plow. Unless you wanted to trudge up the hill, in the sharp quiet air and crunching snow under your feet, all the way into town.

Henrietta wasn't the least bit worried. She knew she'd have no trouble enjoying the quiet. Especially not this year. It would be such a warm, safe, enclosed life. She wouldn't have any complaints. She'd just turn up the oil furnace a little and put a couple of logs in the fire and sit and read, or sit and sew, or eat popcorn and watch TV with Nate. But that was only at night of course. During the cold day, there was still a lot of work to do to get things ready for the chickens. Henrie figured the coops were not in very good condition at all. That was one place Pap had never expended himself, not as far as his building ability. It was funny to live in a builder's house. There was the patio in the back that started off as a grand idea, with a barbecue pit and all but never got finished. Little brick walls were partly built up around it, with unfinished flower boxes. The house inside was mostly done, except for a couple of things she remembered; like the missing marble window sills in the upstairs bedroom and down in Henrietta's room, and the built-in dresser that had a regular dresser stuck in front of the hole where it should have been. Henrie didn't have any illusions about living with a carpenter and having the perfect house. She did hope, though, that it wouldn't be too hard to bring the old coops up to snuff. This first winter could be thin financially. Grandma acted like she had plenty of money, but Henrie knew she couldn't have all that much more than she needed herself. Maybe she had enough to help them get a few repairs done and get a small brood going; a little for feed and scratch and bedding at first. There was going to be so much to do. Henrie wasn't optimistic about Nate finding work right away so soon either. If things could be this hard in California, then they would be even harder in Ohio. She remembered Pap sometimes in the winter, with no work, stomping around the house, finding something wrong with everything, or yelling at drawings in the front study, trying to come up with a way to "get more out of his stick or sheetrock usage," he might say. Grandma tried to keep Henrietta out of the way then, helping her in the kitchen with making Pap a pie to calm him down.

Henrie realized there was plenty for Nate to be afraid of. It wasn't an easy life. But she knew it could be a good one. She was just glad Tommy hadn't come with them. Nate had seemed so interested in helping him.

She was getting what she wanted, but what did Nate want? She wasn't sure he even wanted her. She was beginning to see that he didn't trust things, or maybe he didn't trust her. Seeing this in Nate, she suddenly realized, like seeing a last bright shot of orange sun falling through the mountains, how people usually take a bad thing happening to them as proof of their unsuitability. They think proper judgment has at last been passed and that all their masquerading, all their hiding their lack of value is finally of no more use. Her skin flushed when she thought of how she had abandoned Mary and Bill. She knew she was going to have to write them a letter. She was ashamed of the way she had treated them. Henrietta knew now that a couple of deep hurts could snap the flimsy struts that hold up the faces of our lives. If you took all the people living in crummy hotels, or without food out on the streets, as evidence, then life was truly disintegrating, falling to disrepair, no matter what any newspaper might say. Henrie remembered how Pap used to always say, "You can't stop for a minute. If you do, everything will fall apart on you." As she thought about it too, Grandma didn't spend much time sitting still, doing nothing. If she was talking and sitting, she was always mending or knitting if it was winter time, or shelling beans or shucking corn or something like that if it was summer or fall. Even after Pap died, for the last year Henrie was there, Grandma wouldn't sit still or talk about how she felt. She had a lot more time on her hands, not having to care for him, so she made hats and scarves, and mittens. Henrietta teased her once, joking about who was going to wear all of those.

"They'll find a use, Henrie. Worthwhile things always do."

When Grandma gave them to the church to send off, Henrie was ashamed. For some reason, she came to see that comment of Grandma's as a remark about her. She started measuring herself against it, living with her on the farm, doing nothing really to make a life for herself but helping with the few chickens and the house. It was shameful she knew now, almost three years after Pap died, that Grandma certainly hadn't meant anything about her. It was just the same way Bill and Mary wouldn't have thought badly about her. At least not the way she thought about herself. But to feel a certain way was to be that way, so she had to move out and go somewhere. And besides, how else would she have met Nate?

Henrie had never been much of one to sit and figure things out like this. It was more like Nate. Maybe he was rubbing off on her. But she didn't feel like she was gaining layers. She felt like she was peeling them off herself; like she was getting back to something much less cumbersome.

The train had slowed to a chunking roll. If Nate hadn't been asleep before, he was now. His face was turned toward her, pushed deep into the seat back. He looked to be briefly free of cares and fears. She was grateful for that, for him.

www.ingramcontent.com/pod-product-compliance
Lightning Source LLC
Chambersburg PA
CBHW031536310726
48971CB00008B/2504